Lessons in Logic

LESSONS IN LOGIC

Janie Bolitho

Constable • London

First published in Great Britain 2002
by Constable, an imprint of Constable & Robinson Ltd
3 The Lanchesters, 162 Fulham Palace Road,
London W6 9ER
www.constablerobinson.com

ISBN 1–84119–429–8

Printed and bound in Great Britain

A CIP catalogue record for this book
is available from the British Library

For Jan Carter
(a.k.a. Skippy)

Chapter One

Luke Johnson shook as he stood outside the back entrance of the Chinese takeaway. He was surrounded by black bin liners full of rubbish which were awaiting collection the following morning. From the tiny kitchen came the sound of pans clattering on burners and the scrape of metal utensils. The noises were periodically overridden by the rapid, staccato instructions issuing from the harried woman behind the counter at the front of the shop where customers waited for their meals. Flames shot up the sides of the woks and moist clouds of steam billowed towards the ceiling then settled as the contents of the pans began to simmer. To Luke, the heat in the doorway and the pungency of the aromas wafting through it and mixing with the smell of the rotting rubbish seemed unbearable.

'You'd better not let me down,' the owner said in his strongly accented English as he handed over some money. Not all of it, not by a long way, but enough to cover the expenses Luke said they had already incurred. Jo Chan, like many of his race, was small, no higher than Luke's shoulder, but he was menacing, even in his blue and white checked trousers and the dirty white jacket and headgear he wore. His teeth were stained brown and two of them were missing, his fudge-coloured skin was heavily wrinkled.

'Wednesday, at the latest, as we promised,' Luke responded, stepping backwards, longing to be away from both the place and the awful man in his dirty clothes. But he would have to buy something to take home with him now because his mother could not fail to smell the odours which had permeated his clothes and she would be hurt if she thought he had eaten alone.

He walked down the alley and around to the front entrance. There was now only one person waiting to be served. Luke placed his double order of beef curry and rice and pancake rolls and paid with one of the notes he had just been handed.

Twenty minutes later, having made one quick telephone call from the phone box behind the flats, he handed his mother her plate, dished up his own meal and began to eat even though the food half choked him. He should never have allowed himself to be talked into it but it was too late to back out now. It was Bank Holiday Monday, a day off for most people, but he had had business to attend to and his mother had had to work. The old people she helped care for still needed feeding. She was grateful to him, he knew that, but he wished he could do more for her. Luke had no idea that his mother thought he didn't like her much.

The property had undergone its second transformation since its original construction. Years ago, before the bypass had been built and the Happy Eater had taken away the trade, it had been a petrol station and transport café. The corrugated roof had rusted and weeds grew through the tarmac during the years it had been abandoned. A Chinese family had bought it cheaply and converted it to a pagoda-style restaurant serving top class food and no takeaways. They had made their money and retired.

Julie Watson breathed in the smells of new wood, paint and the hessian fabric which covered the walls. Both external and internal conversions were brilliant and would not have looked out of place in any of the world's capitals. Jim Hurst, the proprietor of La Pêche, had chosen his architect well.

She turned and walked across the thickly carpeted floor to her own domain. The architect had planned the building, Julie had been employed to design the kitchen.

'What sort of food do you intend serving?' Julie had wanted to know at her initial interview after she had submitted her tender.

The question had surprised Jim. 'Why?'

'Because once I've seen a draft menu I can choose the equipment and the placing of it.'

He had watched her from behind his desk in the office, the first room to have been completed, and realized it was an intelligent question.

Julie knew he found her attractive, but she wasn't interested. Mid-fifties, she reckoned, thickish build, medium height, kind, pleasant face but not her type. He had nodded, steepled his hands beneath his chin and told her the job was hers. 'I'll see that you get the information you need within the next couple of days,' he had added, standing to let her know that the interview was at an end.

Fish, mainly, hence the name, she had noticed when the printed menu sheets arrived in the post, but it would never be battered or served with chips. It wasn't that sort of restaurant. No need for a deep fryer in that case. The old kitchen had been ripped out in its entirety as being unsuitable for the change of use.

She stood, surveying her handiwork. A seamless run of stainless steel work surfaces gleamed beneath the bright fluorescent lights; the wall and floor tiles, likewise. The grout had been expensive but came up to environmental health standards, as did everything else, in that it didn't absorb grease and was easy to clean.

The ovens were gas-fired and fitted into the wall, and there were four burners on each of the hobs that formed an island in the centre of the room around which the chefs could move with ease. Knives were slotted into wooden holders which sharpened the blades with each insertion. Stacked on the shelves was a mixture of aluminium, copper and steel pans which Julie knew the chefs would oil or sprinkle with salt then put on the hob or in the oven to blacken before they were used. This would prevent the contents from sticking. She smiled as she recalled the horror on her last employer's face when he learned this would happen. And in the cupboard were the fish kettles which would cover two burners. Whole sea-bass and red mullet would be cooked in these; both were expensive but would provide a meal for two.

She checked the freezers, they were full, as was the cupboard which was designed to hold industrial cleaning materials. She pulled open drawers. Spatulas, fish slices, coring knives and garlic presses. Almost everything on her list was there. It was the first Bank Holiday of May; Jim had invited her to the opening night in less than a week's time. She hoped the food would live up to the kitchen. She also hoped her cheque would soon be forthcoming. Smiling, she turned off the lights. The job was nearly over; after tomorrow she had a few days off in which to relax before she commenced on the next one. She would spend the time paying attention to her own home, a three-bedroomed house she had recently purchased, one of the smaller properties in Maple Grove. Anywhere else in Rickenham Green and it would have cost half the price she had paid but the wide tree-lined street was quiet and it was an address worth the money. The garden surrounding it was what had convinced her to buy it. It was established and needed little work and was not overlooked, except at the front where the double gates stood.

She made certain the building was secure and went out to her car, the only one in the car-park. It was eight o'clock, she'd done enough for one day. Glancing around, the keys already in her hand, Julie unlocked the door and got in. Her life had taken an upward turn. Only one thing bothered her, the telephone calls she had been receiving. Three of them, all late at night. They had woken her up. So far, the police had done nothing.

She started the engine. Checking in her rear-view mirror she caught a quick glimpse of her wide brown eyes and the fringe of her dark, shoulder-length hair as she depressed the clutch and put the car into reverse. I'm paranoid, she thought. Those calls have unsettled me. There's nobody here, there's nobody watching me.

The drive home was uneventful although the traffic was heavier than she had anticipated as people returned from wherever they had been over the holiday weekend. Dusk had fallen by the time she pulled into her drive. The bonnet of the car gleamed under the security light activated by sensors. The hall light glowed through the coloured glass panes in the door. It was on a timing device, an addition purchased since she had started living alone. Matthew had gone. It was the usual sad story, he had met someone younger, a divorce had followed quickly. The shock had worn off, Julie had thrown herself into the work she had done half-heartedly when Matt had supported her. And now she had made a name for herself.

Inside the house she exhaled with relief, unaware how nervous she had been walking from the garage to the front door. She checked every room, throwing on lights as she did so. All was quiet, all was safe. The indicator on the answering-machine remained static, there were no messages. Good. She poured a brandy and added soda then kicked off her shoes and sat down. Spring had arrived, and with it had come more offers of work. That was enough to be going on with, her personal life would fall into place later. I'll join the gym and do all those things women's magazines advise singles to do, she thought, wondering if she was hungry enough to be bothered to cook. Matthew has his new life, I shall have mine. The house is a start. All I need now is to make some new friends.

She walked through to her own kitchen which she might one day redesign. Julie was unsure whether or not she liked the terracotta colour scheme. Although the quarry-tiled floor was easy to clean it would be cold in the winter. There was plenty of time, she had her whole life ahead of her. Her new life. One which didn't include Matthew, but nonetheless her own. She was, after all, only thirty. It was as well they had postponed having children, although she had wanted them.

11

The telephone rang. She held her breath, waiting for the machine to kick in. If it was the obscene caller he wouldn't leave a message, she was sure of that. It was too risky, he'd know she could take the tape to the police who had told her they might be able to use it as a form of voice identification.

'Are you there, Julie? It's Jim Hurst. I've just been to La Pêche. I can't tell you how pleased I am with what you've achieved. Anyway, see you on Friday. 'Bye. Oh, you can let me have the keys back then.'

She let the tape play. Although she didn't mind checking on things on a Bank Holiday it had been an exhausting couple of months and she was too tired to pick up the phone and hold a conversation with him, but from the brief message it obviously wasn't necessary.

Tomorrow night she would return to the restaurant for the last time before it opened. The dining-room furniture, linens, cutlery, glasses and crockery were all being delivered along with some special vegetable steamers and a few extra items she had considered necessary for the kitchen. Nothing must go wrong if she was to keep her reputation. She would do as Jim said; make her final check tomorrow while there was still time to purchase anything that was missing, then hand him back the keys on Friday.

Two hours later she slid her thin frame between the sheets. She smiled as she turned out the light. For someone who spent her working life designing kitchens, she wasn't much of a cook. Scrambled eggs and smoked salmon might be all right for breakfast, but it hadn't been much of a dinner.

At ten past one the telephone rang.

Gregory Grant was tired and frustrated. The man sitting opposite him still claimed to be innocent.

'Look, I know her, I don't know why she's doing this,'

he'd repeated. That, and 'No, I don't know anything about the others.'

But Maggie Telford had managed to keep him talking long enough for them to trace the call while her new boyfriend had rung them on his mobile. Anthony Peter Smithson had been picked up by two patrol officers just as he was leaving the public telephone booth.

There was not enough evidence to hold him. If he had been responsible for those other calls there was no way in which they could prove it. Smithson was allowed to go. Maybe the long session in the interview room would serve to deter him in future. He had been released at 21.43 on the Bank Holiday Monday.

Detective Sergeant Gregory Grant squeezed his eyelids between thumb and forefinger, wondering if he'd returned to work too soon. No, he'd been given the all-clear by his GP. His appendix had been removed and the small scar had healed quickly and satisfactorily. He felt out of place, that was all. He was new to the area and didn't know anyone yet.

DC Brenda Gibbons sat beside him, deep in her own thoughts. She had worked the case, interviewing the women who had been on the receiving end of obscene telephone calls, but he wasn't sure what to make of her. She showed no signs of revulsion towards Smithson, but no sympathy either. Greg was surprised but impressed with her professional attitude.

Smithson was not on any list of sex offenders and he had no previous record of any description. Maybe he'd been lucky in the past.

Half a dozen women had reported receiving these calls over a period of several months. Two of them also believed they were being followed. 'It's just a feeling,' Maggie Telford had told them the first time she complained. 'But the calls are real enough.'

All of the women had three things in common: they lived alone, they were aged between twenty-five and thirty, and they had long, dark hair.

'It's usually blondes they go for,' Brenda said, as if she had been reading his mind.

Greg glanced at her shiny long hair. Copper or chestnut? he asked himself as it gleamed under the ceiling lights. Brenda Gibbons ought to be safe from Smithson. Greg's wife had been blonde, naturally so. 'Do you believe him?'

Brenda met the eyes of the new Detective Sergeant. There were dark circles beneath them and his skin was greyish. Prior to his arrival they had joked about his name, Gregory Grant, and pictured film star looks. How wrong they had been. Beside her sat a man in his late forties with slightly greasy hair already turning grey. His features were large and ill matched yet he wasn't ugly. It was a comfortable, lived-in sort of face, a bit like an older version of DC Eddie Roberts. His body was lean and firm and he dressed well but he seemed to lack vitality. Recently convalescent, he might not have completely regained his health. They knew little about the man yet, he'd only joined them three days ago. 'I don't know. He was caught in the act, why not hold his hand up to the others? He must know it would make it easier for him in the long run.

'Anyway, we'll see if any more complaints come in. We might've scared him off. ' She stood. 'Fancy a coffee? I need one before I push off.' She had a ten-mile drive to face and her eyes felt gritty.

The look of gratitude in his eyes spoke volumes. He's lonely, she thought. New job, new town, no wonder.

'I'd love one.'

The interview tapes had been sealed and despatched to Records. They left the room, descended a flight of concrete stairs and turned the corner of the basement corridor. Ahead were the swing doors of the canteen with their plastic porthole windows which reminded Brenda of the old-fashioned doors in some hospital wards.

A few of the tables were occupied and some desultory conversation was taking place but no one was laughing. It was that time of night. The uniformed back shift were out on patrol and most of their fellow detectives had already left. Anyone present was either having a late supper because there was no one at home to cook for or to cook for them, or they were there in advance of the night shift, stoking up on fat and carbohydrate to see them through the small hours.

Brenda bought their coffees and carried them to a formica-topped table which was smeared with brown sauce. They sat beneath the bright, unflattering fluorescent lights. Despite the extractor fans the air was redolent with the smell of chips and bacon sandwiches.

'Thanks.' Greg reached for the bowl containing packets of sugar, ripped off the corner of two of them and poured the contents into his mug, stirring slowly and smoothly as he did so. He picked it up and sipped the lukewarm coffee which had sat on the filter machine for far too long. He seemed unsure how to begin a conversation.

'Have you settled in yet, sir?' Brenda finally asked, wondering why she hadn't simply gone home as she'd longed to do.

'No, not yet. The house is smaller than our previous one, there's a lot of weeding out of furniture to be done. I expect my daughter'll be glad of some of it. She got married recently.' He lowered his grey eyes. 'Greg will do,' he said, slightly embarrassed, unsure of the protocol at Rickenham Green. It varied from station to station.

'Brenda then.' She smiled. 'Where is your house?'

'On the Bradley estate. It suits me, they're easy to care for.'

She noted the use of pronouns. Our previous house. It suits me. Was there a recent divorce in his background? Was that the reason for the lugubrious expression? Perhaps his daughter had lived with him and now she had left home he had moved to a smaller place. She did not know him well enough to ask. She turned the conversation back to the job. 'This Smithson, have you had time to read through all the reports?'

'Yes. He doesn't seem to fit the usual profile.'

'I know. Surely he had the sense to realize that the longer he spoke the more chance there was of us catching him?

15

That makes me wonder if he is telling the truth, if he's only responsible for the calls to Maggie Telford as he says. Maybe she really does know him.'

'Which she denies.'

Brenda's hair had fallen over one shoulder. She brushed it back with a sweep of her hand. 'I wonder if reporting these incidents in the *Rickenham Herald* was wise?'

'Copycat crime?'

Brenda took a sip of coffee then put down her mug. It was impossible to drink the rest of its stewed contents. 'Possibly. Except Maggie Telford fits the description of the other victims and the fact that they look alike wasn't mentioned in the press release.'

Detective Superintendent Thorne had taken some time in deciding whether or not to go to the press. If it scared off the perpetrator the women would have nothing more to fear, but neither would they catch him. The main advantage in releasing the details was to warn women and to advise them what to do if it happened to them.

The article had not scared Smithson, or else he had not read it.

'He's got a full-time job in insurance,' Grant said, 'he's buying his own flat, he's presentable and he's sustained long-term relationships with women over the years. Or so he tells us.'

'That's what puzzles me,' Brenda replied. This wasn't some inadequate, some mother-dominated figure they were dealing with. A preliminary check on his background had produced nothing adverse.

'Well, I think I'll make a move.' Brenda glanced at the clock on the canteen wall. Ten fifteen, she'd be home by quarter to eleven and Andrew would be waiting for her. What, she wondered, did Greg Grant have to go home to?

Chapter Two

'Go and have a bath. You'll only moan you're stiff in the morning if you don't,' Moira said. Not long having come out of the shower herself, she now sat in her nightclothes on a chair covered with a dust sheet and sipped a glass of wine.

The bay windows were open but the evening was becoming chilly. The first week of May had arrived, the Bank Holiday weekend, and Ian had used it to start decorating the living-room. The spare bedroom and bathroom had been completed some time ago. Moira had imagined his new interest would fade as rapidly as it had appeared but she had been wrong.

The furniture was pushed to the centre of the room, draped in old curtains, and the room was harshly lit by the unshaded bulbs of the overhead light fitting. Against one wall lay the rolled-up carpet. Only three days had passed since Ian had begun but Moira wondered how much longer she could stand living in such conditions. However, Ian seemed happy and they had spent the weekend in domestic harmony at home, even if not together for most of the time. She had worked in the garden tidying up the daffodils; tulips had replaced them now, and wallflowers. Their new lightweight mower had made cutting the dry grass easy, and she had planted runner beans.

Tomorrow Ian would return to work, as would she, and, hopefully, he would return in the evening to finish the papering then things could get back to normal.

The telephone rang. Ian frowned as he glanced at his

watch. 'I'll get it,' he said, aware of the calls women had been receiving at night. It almost eleven. It had to be work or bad news.

'It was Mark,' he said a few minutes later. Mark, their son, was now married to Yvette and living in Italy where they both scraped a living as artists. 'That boy's got no regard for time. He sounded as lively as if he'd just got up. Do you suppose they actually have a siesta? Anyway, they want to come over in the summer.'

'I hope you said they could.'

Ian nodded, wondering what his daughter-in-law would think of their home. The Dupois family, her family, was extremely wealthy. Then he wondered why it should matter.

'You're tired. Go on, go and have that bath.' Moira got up to close the windows then sat down to finish her drink. Yes, it had been a nice weekend, they'd even eaten lunch in the garden. Spring was her favourite time of year. A time of hope. But not for those women Ian had mentioned, she realized. How awful to live alone and have someone whispering obscenities to you late at night. Having an unlisted number was no protection. Their own number wasn't in the book but people still managed to get hold of it.

Yawning, she pulled the curtains, switched off the light and closed the door to prevent the smell of gloss paint from permeating the whole house. She heard the bath water run down the pipes as she got into bed, aching a little herself from her outdoor efforts.

They awoke to another bright and sunny morning. As she made tea Moira surveyed the garden from the kitchen window. Despite the bitter easterly winds which had swept across the North Sea and over Suffolk during the winter, the geraniums had survived in their sheltered garden. Some were already in bud.

The stairs creaked beneath Ian's feet. He was a big man, six feet four, and therefore was able to carry a little extra weight but he struggled to keep it down. With Moira's help and positive encouragement he mostly managed.

'My back's creasing me,' he said as he lowered himself into a kitchen chair.

Moira smirked but said nothing. She rarely got a 'good morning' or a 'hello'. His first daily words of greeting usually consisted of an update on his current minor ailment. She handed him a low-fat yogurt and a spoon and placed a banana beside his mug of tea. 'I'm going to get dressed,' she said as she passed him on her way out of the door.

Ian had enjoyed his days off. Despite a few mild aches he felt fitter for the hard work. And sunshine helped. It had flooded the house and he had soaked it up in the garden when he had stopped for tea or beer. Not hot sunshine, but with enough warmth to penetrate clothing. No one had contacted him from work. Friday had been a quiet day; he hoped it had stayed that way over the weekend.

They left the house and walked part of the way together, preferring to ignore the car when the weather was good. Ian would carry on towards the town centre, Moira turned left into Saxborough Road at the top of the High Street. She worked in the offices of a car showroom, one which sold top-of-the-range vehicles.

Ian waved and blew her a kiss as she walked away, thinking anew how young she looked in her dress and jacket with her fair hair moving across her shoulders in the mild breeze. She might have been twenty years his junior, not fifteen.

'Any luck with the obscene caller?' Detective Chief Inspector Ian Roper asked when he finally encountered Brenda Gibbons on Tuesday afternoon.

Brenda explained what had happened then shrugged. 'We had to let Smithson go. He didn't deny ringing Maggie

Telford but he claims he wasn't responsible for the other calls.'

'And?' They began to walk towards the general office from which the detectives worked if they were not assigned to other jobs. Ian had been in a policy meeting all morning and wanted to catch up on the events of the weekend.

'And I think I believed him, sir. I think Greg did, too.'

Greg, not Sergeant Grant, Ian noticed. Brenda hadn't wasted much time in getting to know their new member. His references were excellent but Ian had found him a little cold on the two occasions they had met. Maybe not cold but aloof, which could mean shy. Still, there was a reason for that. It was only a year since his wife had died and he must be lonelier still now that his daughter had married and left home. Perhaps the change of scene would do him good. 'So where are you going from here?' he continued.

'I'm going to speak to all six women again. He has to have met them to know how similar they look.'

'Is there any other connection? Between the women, I mean. For instance do they all go to evening classes or belong to the same club or gym?'

'That's what we're going to establish next. Until we started interviewing we had no idea they all had long, dark hair. We only realized yesterday that these probably aren't random calls.'

'Fine. I'll let you get on with it then.'

DCs Alan Campbell and Eddie Roberts were nowhere to be seen and the general office was almost deserted. The station still had a holiday feel to it but maybe that was more to do with the welcome spring sunshine which lit the modern building through its many large windows than the fact that the room was almost empty. It had been a long, miserable winter.

It was Detective Inspector Short who gave him a run-down of the weekend. Nothing startling, nothing big had occurred, nothing to raise Ian's blood pressure. He had stopped getting worked up over petty crime and mindless violence, things which he could not prevent. The world had changed, the best he could do was to hope that the perpetrators were caught.

'Pretty quiet all round,' Short concluded.

John Short; Scruffy Short. Did he know that was how his colleagues referred to him? Probably, Ian thought, not that he would care. He had never met a man so comfortable with himself and his life, so able to take anything and everything in his stride and retain a sense of humour; not a sense of humour everyone appreciated but there all the same. That his personal hygiene could have been better and some of his habits were less than salubrious seemed inconsequential to the man. Ian had come to accept that he was now one of the team. He showed no signs of moving on even though his appointment was supposed to have been temporary. And Superintendent Thorne was keeping remarkably quiet on the subject.

Brenda Gibbons reappeared bearing a tray of tea. Always fresh, always clean, she was the perfect antithesis to Short. She was dressed in cream trousers and a matching blouse, both of which were spotless. Her shiny hair was tied in a pony-tail and her toenails, showing through cork-heeled sandals, were painted a dusky pink. She nudged aside some paperwork and placed the tray on her desk.

'I've arranged a further interview with all six women,' she said as she handed around the mugs. 'I'm seeing two of them this afternoon and the others tomorrow. Oh, and Julie Watson's received another phone call. She's already reported several of them.'

'When did she get it? Today?' Short stroked his straggling moustache. If so, it was the first one to have been received in the daytime.

'No. It was late last night but she wasn't sure whether to bother us again as we already knew about the others.'

'But she changed her mind.'

'Yes.' Brenda winced as Short slurped his tea. Drops

21

adhered to his moustache. 'She thought it best to tell us because she had a feeling she was being watched.'

'Just like the Telford woman.'

'She used more or less the same words. She couldn't be sure, she hadn't actually seen anyone.' But they were all aware that feelings should not be ignored. 'Anyway, I'll be speaking to her in the morning.' Brenda looked at her notes. At four o'clock she had an appointment with Pam Richards and, after that, another with Cassandra Maguire.

The sun had moved westwards and the general office was now in partial shadow but it was still warm, unusually warm for early May. Ian, in shirt-sleeves, decided to return to his own office and deal with whatever was in his in-tray. With luck he could get away early and finish the decorating.

Pam Richards was a freelance window-dresser and was suitably remunerated for her talent. Her work took her to stores throughout East Anglia and sometimes to London or further afield. It allowed her imagination plenty of scope. She had just returned from Ipswich where she had been discussing ideas with a store manager. She often dressed windows at night, when the stores were empty, but meetings concerning her ideas had to take place in the daytime. She had told Brenda she would be at home any time after three thirty.

Brenda parked outside the small cottage which was about three miles from the town centre. The cottage was nearer to Little Endesley, an outlying village, than to Rickenham Green but her address, thanks to the mysterious ways of the Post Office, was the latter.

The small front garden was bright with spring flowers and honeysuckle trailed around the trellis-work which formed the porch. The only sounds were birdsong until Brenda rapped the metal knocker against the door. The birds stopped singing and silence ensued. There were no signs of life apart from a newish car parked on the verge in the lane. The upstairs windows were open, the ones on the ground floor were not.

There was the sound of a bolt being drawn and the door opened. 'I knew it was you. I saw you get out of the car. Come in, I've just made some tea.'

Pam Richards was about five feet four, the same height as Brenda, but stockier. Brenda looked at her closely. Apart, the women in question might have been sisters but placed together their differences would be more noticeable.

She was shown into a front room in keeping with the exterior of the cottage. An open fireplace held a copper jug of dried grasses, there was chintz at the windows and a comfortable-looking suite upholstered in the palest of greens.

'Do sit down, I won't be a second. Do you take sugar?'

'No, thanks.'

Pam Richards disappeared to the kitchen. Brenda admired the room in her absence. It was homely and lived in rather than something which owed its taste to an interior decorator. There were books on the shelves and ornaments which looked more personal than valuable. But the cottage was isolated, set back from the main road and easily approachable from over the fields behind it. The pleasure of living there must have been marred by the fear of unwanted telephone calls.

Pam returned carrying two hand-painted earthenware mugs, one of which she handed to Brenda. She was wearing jeans and a blouse and must have changed since her business appointment in Ipswich. Her dark hair hung down her back. It was parted on one side with a half fringe. She was more stunning than beautiful.

'There haven't been any more calls, just the two,' she began.

'Good. But we do need some more details. You see, we think it's possible that you've met this man or, at least, that he's seen you somewhere.'

23

Pam sat down heavily. 'What makes you say that? I assumed he'd picked my number from the book at random and got lucky when a female answered. I'm listed as P. Richards.'

'We don't think so. The other women, they have things in common with you.'

Pam's face was white and her hand shook as she sipped her tea. 'What things?'

'You've all got long dark hair and live alone and you're all within the same age group. What we'd like is for you to make a list of all visitors to the house over the past couple of months; repair men, meter readers, friends and relations, anyone at all. Also a list of any clubs or societies you belong to. Include anyone at all you can think of with whom you come into contact, whether regularly or not.' From the nature of Pam's work Brenda did not think it likely that a connection stemmed from there. Her movements were unpredictable and it was doubtful that the five other women shopped in all the stores in Suffolk and Norfolk and elsewhere whose windows Pam dressed. The link had to be nearer home, probably in Rickenham Green.

'Shall I do it now?'

'No. Give yourself some time to think about it.'

Pam nodded. 'It won't be difficult, I keep a careful diary because of my job.'

Brenda stood. 'Just let me know when you've completed it.' She hesitated, about to ask if Pam, too, felt she was being watched, but she was scared enough already and seemed to be taking sensible precautions as far as security was concerned. 'Thank you for the tea.'

Pam came with her to the door. Brenda heard the bolt slide across behind her. How awful not to be able to open the downstairs windows on such a lovely afternoon for fear someone might enter that way.

The heady scent of sun-warmed wallflowers filled the air. In another month it would be overtaken by that of the honeysuckle. Spiraea bushes, growing against the fence at the side, lent a misty aura to the plants growing in front of them. It was a real cottage garden. Brenda's own garden at the house she now shared with Andrew Osborne was nowhere near as pretty. It was too close to the coastline, open to the winter gales and salt-laden breezes, for anything other than hardy shrubs to flourish. But it didn't matter. The large, stone house itself was lovely and she had Andrew who had made her forget her dismal childhood and a short-lived violent marriage.

Brenda got into the car, negotiated a three-point turn and headed back towards Rickenham Green. Pam Richards would not take any risks, Brenda was certain of that. Cassandra Maguire might be a different matter.

The maisonette, one in a block of eight, was near the town centre. The block had been purpose-built in the late seventies and reflected the architecture of the time. The lines were severe but had the redeeming feature of large windows which protruded from the building forming bays which rested one on the other, thus breaking the harshness of the design.

Brenda mounted the concrete steps at the back and pressed the bell, which rang shrilly. Through the star-patterned double-glazed door she saw the thin figure of Cassandra Maguire hurrying to admit her.

'Hi. Come in.' She turned away immediately, leaving Brenda to close the door.

The place smelled of furniture polish and disinfectant. Either Cassandra Maguire had been spring-cleaning or she had a regular cleaner.

Cassandra swung around to face her. Vibrant, Brenda thought, or full of nervous energy, but her rapid movements were not due to fear, she was not as scared as Pamela Richards. Which meant she was likely to take more chances. The front windows were wide open but as the lower floor of this particular maisonette was two storeys up and the door was at the back of the property no one would attempt to get in via those windows.

'Drink?' She spoke as she moved, with the minimum of waste.

'No, thanks.'

Cassandra picked up a glass. She had started early. They both sat down. Cassandra reached for her cigarettes and lighter. 'I'm not sure that I can tell you anything new. I've no idea who this man is and I certainly didn't recognize the voice. I might be wrong but it didn't seem as if he was trying to disguise it either. What he said was, well, disgusting, but nothing out of the ordinary if you know what I mean, nothing terribly inventive. Just what he'd like to do to me and how much I'd enjoy it and that one day, if I was lucky, it would happen. Call me Cass, by the way. Everyone does.'

Brenda repeated the request she had made to Pam Richards. In looks the women were alike, but they differed widely in manner. Pam's actions were smooth and fluid, Cass's were jerky and fast. Her dark hair was tied back in a pony-tail exposing well-defined bones and an enviably smooth forehead.

'Yeah, I can soon make a list. It shouldn't be difficult, hardly anyone ever comes here.' She grinned. 'I'm lazy and I'm a lousy cook. I do all my entertaining out. Are you sure you won't have a drink?'

Brenda declined as Cass got up to pour herself another one. Presumably this was her usual routine as it seemed to have no visible effects.

The room was L-shaped, the longer arm leading to the window, the shorter to the right of it. The window recess held a desk upon which were magazines and a computer. It was where Cass worked. She was a freelance journalist, writing articles for magazines on cosmetics. Odd that she wore none herself, but her skin was a good advertisement for whatever she used on it. Brenda wondered if this was another connection. Not where the women worked but the type of work they did. Pam was a freelance window-dresser, Cass a freelance journalist. And Julie Watson designed kitchens. It was her own business, she, too, was self-employed and she worked alone. These women presented a certain image: confident, well off and in a different league from many of the victims they encountered. Unable to recall how the other three women earned a living, she made a mental note to check.

Like Pam, Cass promised to make the list that evening. Neither had made plans to go out; neither, at that point, was involved with a man, although both had been in relationships at various times. It might or might not be relevant.

Brenda returned to her car which was parked in one of the maisonette bays. She made a brief visit to the station then drove the ten miles home to where, hopefully, Andrew would be waiting. He had not mentioned any court cases or late appointments so, with any luck, they could spend the evening together. It was a rare occurrence lately. She smiled. The Chief might call him an ugly brute but Brenda had always been able to see that beneath the pock-marked face and slightly hunched shoulders of a man who had been self-conscious of his height in youth, there was a decent, caring man who had come to love her and whom she loved in return.

She turned off the coast road and swung into the lane which led to the house. With a sigh of relief she saw that Andrew's car was already parked in the spacious drive.

On Tuesday evening Luke Johnson and Terry Noble were on the road leading to Aldeburgh. Terry was driving an unmarked blue van with mud smeared over the registration plates. Ahead was a clean red Citroën, driven by a woman. She indicated left. Terry slowed down and swore when he saw where she was heading, then he pulled into the side of the road.

The woman got out of the car and locked it and made her way towards the side entrance of the restaurant where she let herself in with a key.

'What do we do now?' Luke asked, fear turning his stomach to water.

Terry grinned. 'There's ways around everything.'

'But it's Tuesday now and we promised . . .'

'Keep your hair on, Luke, it's Jo Chan we're talking about, not some member of the Triads.' He tapped the steering wheel, frowning in concentration. 'There's only one thing we can do, isn't there?' he said.

Luke nodded. He guessed what it would be and that disaster lay ahead. Nothing was working out in the way in which it was supposed to and they were sure to be caught.

Chapter Three

Maggie Telford had had a long day. It was Tuesday. The first day back at work after a long weekend always seemed more tiring. Because she always wanted to be at her best for him she regretted inviting Brian over for dinner. It was too late to put him off now as he would have already left Saxborough.

She had showered, changed into a silvery silk shirt, black crêpe trousers and Italian sandals then brushed her long dark hair until it crackled before twisting it behind her head and securing it with a tortoiseshell clip.

Dinner would now be simple rather than the more elaborate meal she had planned. The steak would be grilled and eaten with salad instead of cooked in a green pepper sauce and served with vegetables. She had cheated on the starter and bought ready-made crab cakes and an accompanying sauce. If Brian was still hungry there was always cheese or fruit to follow.

Maggie had been seeing Brian Schofield for almost a month. He was an enigmatic man, one whose thoughts she could never guess at. He intrigued her. He was certainly attractive, easy to be with, witty and intelligent. It was early days yet but, unusually, he had made no attempt to get her into bed. Some men had tried it on their first date.

She had just opened the red wine to allow it to breathe when the telephone rang. Licking a finger she had dipped in the redcurrant sauce she had decanted into a glass dish, she went to answer it.

'I'll be a bit late, Maggie. Something came up which I had to sort out. We can go out if you prefer.'

'No. Everything's ready here. How long do you think you'll be?'

'No more than half an hour. I'll see you soon.'

Maggie hung up, thankful that she hadn't gone to more trouble or the food would have been ruined. She poured some wine and sat by the open window of her Edwardian house which looked out on to the deserted street. Only a couple of feet of paving stones and some tall iron railings separated her from the pavement. The scent of the flowers she had planted in tubs drifted towards her. A single car passed and a bee droned in the potted lavender plant. She might almost have been in the country. The house was situated in a crescent, there was no reason for anyone to use the road unless they lived there or were visiting someone. It had been left to her parents by her grandmother but as they already owned a place in the Cotswolds and another in London, they had transferred the deeds to Maggie. She appreciated she was luckier than most. She had health and good looks, no mortgage to worry about and a well-paid job as a partner in a dental practice. Men had never been a problem until she had made the mistake of marrying one. This marriage, to a fellow dentist called Mark Hopkins, had lasted less than a year. Within months it had become obvious that all they had in common was their respective careers. Their parting had been as amicable as was possible under such circumstances, mainly because they each had enough money to enable them to get on with their lives rather than drag things out with solicitors. Neither had made any claims upon the other and Maggie had immediately reverted to her maiden name. But that was in the past. She was thirty now and had matured. She had rushed into marriage once, she would not make the same mistake again. The last man she had dated had pressurized her, demanded more of her than she was prepared to give. He had had to go but had taken more getting rid of than she had anticipated.

Now there was Brian Schofield, who was not pressurizing her in the least. She smiled. Maybe tonight she would act the feminist and seduce him.

It was eight thirty when he arrived, not much later than the half-hour he had predicted. Maggie appreciated the courtesy of the call.

'I'm so sorry,' he said, kissing the tip of her nose. 'Problems with the staff.'

She smiled at him. He looked hot and exhausted but this did not detract from his good looks. They were opposites, she so dark with an olive complexion and brown eyes, Brian a little taller than her with soft blond hair and eyes of an unusual shade of green. 'You look as if you could do with a drink.'

'I'd love one.' He sank into the leather armchair in which Maggie had been sitting. 'I can't believe how warm it is.' He loosened the tie which went with the suit he wore for work.

'I know. I hope it lasts. But it'll probably pour down in June like it usually does.'

Maggie handed him a brandy and soda. The meal could wait, it would only take minutes to cook. Brian needed a chance to unwind and maybe to tell her what the problem had been that had caused the lines in his face to deepen.

He accepted the drink and stared at the ornate mantelpiece. On it were framed photographs of Maggie's parents and herself and her brother at various stages in their development.

Maggie leaned back into the settee and sipped her own drink. 'What was the trouble about?'

Brian sighed. 'It was all so stupid. It could easily have been sorted out without my being there. There was an argument. One of the waitresses has left and two others were almost coming to blows over who got the overtime until we could find a replacement. I had to stay because they were both threatening to walk out and the restaurant was already serving. They finally agreed to split the hours fifty-fifty which they could have done from the start.

31

'Anyway, let's forget my work. How was your day?'

'Busy.' She grinned. 'But at least my clients can't complain whilst I'm treating them. I'm hungry. Let me see to the food. Come and talk to me in the kitchen.'

Brian watched as she dry-fried the crab cakes and set them on plates already garnished with salad leaves. Yes, on this occasion she had cheated but she was a good cook. She wondered how she compared with the chef at the hotel where Brian was the general manager.

Later, when they had eaten, Maggie stacked the dishwasher and they moved from the dining-room back to the lounge with coffee and brandies. It was dark now but the room was warmly lit by red-shaded table lamps. Brian sat beside her and draped one arm across her shoulders. She leaned closer. He smelled nice, of warm skin and something lemony. He was thirty-eight, not far off a decade older than her. She wondered how he had spent all those years before she had met him, quite by chance, in the Crown one evening. All she knew was that, like herself, he had a brief marriage behind him.

Unexpectedly, he pulled her closer and kissed her. It was unlike the brotherly kisses she had so far experienced. Maggie sensed her seduction skills would not be required that evening . . .

'I never thanked you properly,' she said later, as they lay side by side in her double bed.

Brian turned his head on the pillow and grinned. 'I was under the impression that what we did was a joint effort.'

Maggie grinned back and punched his shoulder gently. 'I meant for last night.'

'Oh that. Forget it.' He turned away as if he was vaguely annoyed.

'But you were so quick thinking.' The moment she had answered the phone and mouthed it was the unwanted caller he had rung the police from his mobile.

'So were you, you kept him talking. I don't think he'll

bother you any more. Come here.' He pulled her to him and kissed her again.

Maggie glanced at the clock. It was late and she had appointments from 8 a.m. The practice only accepted private clients and some of them believed that their businesses could not run without their presence. They wanted appointments early or late. She closed her eyes. The police had informed her that they had arrested Anthony Smithson but she had no idea of the outcome, whether he had been charged with anything or not. As Brian had said, hopefully the calls would cease now.

Jim Hurst had overseen the delivery of the furniture, linens and crockery on Tuesday morning. The former had been arranged in the alcoves and down the centre of the dining-room, the starched tablecloths and serviettes were in a cupboard and the crockery was now stacked in the new storage spaces in the kitchen. There had also been two boxes of kitchen equipment which he had left for Julie to check when she arrived later that day.

On Wednesday morning he drove to La Pêche to have one final look before the opening on Friday. Whilst he was there he would write out a cheque for Julie for services rendered. She had done such a good job that he wanted to settle her account immediately. Besides, he liked to keep his dealings straight and rarely kept anyone waiting for payment. Her neatly presented invoice was lying on his desk.

Jim strolled across the car-park enjoying the feel of the sun on his head. The unseasonally warm weather was a good omen. Julie's car was there, she must also have left her final visit until now. He glanced at the banks of polyanthus in their raised beds and, satisfied that the exterior was as welcoming as the restaurant, walked around to the front of the building where he unlocked the plate-glass double doors and stepped into the dining-room.

He surveyed his new enterprise. Already he could picture the gleaming cutlery and glassware on the white damask tablecloths. He crossed the room. At the back, on the right, was a short corridor leading to the toilets. Like everything else, these had been altered and refurbished. Beyond the corridor was the door to his office, marked Private. To his left were the swing doors to the kitchen. It was surprisingly quiet, maybe Julie was in the Ladies. He pushed a swing door open, then froze. Who would now benefit from his cheque? was his first illogical thought. Not Julie Watson, that much was certain.

She lay on the floor in a pool of congealed blood. One of the knives she had carefully chosen was stuck in her back. Her handbag lay on the floor, its contents strewn over what had been the pristine floor tiles.

Jim Hurst turned away, grabbing the doorpost for support as he felt his legs buckle. His stomach rebelled at what he had seen, he rushed to the toilet and leaned over one of the bowls, gagging drily. The spasm passed. He splashed his face with cold water, washed his hands as though they were contaminated and went to his office to phone the police.

Inspector John Short groaned. He had been happily doing as little as possible while he drank milky coffee and ate chocolate digestives. Crumbs still adhered to his moustache as he pulled on his jacket, the lapels of which didn't quite cover the coffee stain on his shirt.

He and DC Campbell were to attend the scene of the crime. Brenda Gibbons was interviewing the remaining women on her list; there had been four, she did not yet know there were now only three. Eddie Roberts was tidying up the paperwork on a recently solved case and Greg Grant was familiarizing himself with the unsolved cases still on their books. The Chief had been informed and, surprisingly, was not going to take a look for himself. An inspector usually took charge initially, but Ian liked to be present if possible. However, it was known that Super-intendent Thorne wished to speak to him.

Short and Alan Campbell left the building and went out into the sunshine. It was the sort of day when no one should die, certainly not of unnatural causes. They got into the car and made their way towards La Pêche which was situated on the road half-way between Rickenham Green and Aldeburgh.

'They say the sun only shines on the righteous. It's stopped shining on this one, whatever she was like.'

Alan Campbell ignored Short. His eternal use of clichés was either a source of exasperation or the cause of mirth, depending upon the mood of his fellow officers. 'A woman has been murdered.' He knew he sounded priggish but Short brought out the worst in most of them.

'Yeah, well, I always thought that's what the phrase "suspicious death" meant. There're no flies on me, son.' Unperturbed, Short sat back and spent the rest of the journey picking his nose.

Ian had watched them go. It was not from morbid curiosity he wished he was with them. He simply liked to be at the scene, to get a feel for a case. But Mike Thorne was waiting.

Thorne sat behind his desk looking worried. The sun-light which backlit him emphasized the lack of hair on the top of his head. 'Have a seat, Ian,' he said in his West Midlands accent. It had become diluted a little since his sojourn in Suffolk, but he would never lose the nasal twang. 'You know who she is, this woman.'

It was a statement, but Ian shook his head. Short had informed him that the victim was female, that was all.

'Julie Watson.'

It took a few seconds for Ian to realize the significance of the name. It was one he had heard recently. Julie Watson was one of the women who had been receiving those calls. Had Short been particularly awkward by withholding the name or had he failed to realize the significance himself? Whatever the answer, Ian would not have been surprised.

Short was, to use one of his own phrases, a law unto himself.

'Shit.' He shook his head again. 'Sorry, sir.' Thorne had asked him to call him Mike in the privacy of his office but Ian found it hard to do so. 'We let him go.'

'Smithson. Yes, I know.'

The implications of this were enormous. The press and the public would react hysterically if Smithson was guilty. It was bound to come out, it always did. 'DC Gibbons is in the process of interviewing the women again. I'd better get in touch with her.' Julie Watson was no longer available to answer any questions.

'Bring him in again, but go easy.'

'The victim, she reported another call yesterday.'

'Step it up then, Ian, use whatever resources you need. I'll be behind you. If he's killed one . . .' He didn't complete the sentence, they were both aware of what they might be dealing with.

Janice King was twenty-seven but looked younger. Her body was supple, her walk bouncy, which caused her dark hair to swing around her shoulders as she led Brenda to a small room at the back of the hairdresser's where she worked. 'We can talk out here,' she said above the noise of the dryers, conversations and Radio 1. The room smelled even more strongly of the chemicals used in the dyes and the perms which were stored there than the salon itself had done. 'I'm sorry it has to be here but at least I don't have a customer for half an hour. My place is a tip. The man upstairs let his bath overflow and the landlord's in there with builders this morning. I just hope he pays for the decorating afterwards.'

Decorating. Builders. Maybe the other women had used the same firm at some point. Later she would check. 'Here's fine.' There wasn't much room but there was a chair each. Brenda went through the routine again. Janice was saying she would start making a list immediately when Brenda's phone rang. 'Excuse me,' she said, taking it from her leather shoulder-bag. 'I see,' she said quietly, hoping the tremor of panic she felt didn't show. 'Yes. I'll do what I can.'

'Is something wrong?' Janice had seen the detective's expression change.

'Yes, there is. Look, Janice, we'll be keeping an eye on you as best we can, but you've got to be extra careful. Is there anyone you can stay with for a while?'

'Why?' Her eyes widened with fear.

Brenda sighed and ran a hand through her hair. 'One of the other women, she's been killed, ' she said quietly. 'Now we don't . . .' But whatever else she was saying was drowned by Janice's screech of horror.

Another woman rushed to the back of the shop. 'Is everything all right?' she asked, some styling tongs still in her hand.

'Yes.' Brenda was on her feet, one hand on Janice's shoulder. 'Yes, she'll be all right in a minute.'

'Bad news, is it?'

She was in her element, obviously dying to pick up some gossip. Seemingly Janice hadn't confided in her or she would have known the purpose of a visit from the police. Brenda was not going to give her the satisfaction of answering the question. The woman didn't move for several seconds. Only when she realized she would learn nothing did she nod and walk away.

It was another fifteen minutes before Brenda felt able to leave Janice. By then arrangements had been made for her to stay with her brother and his wife. He had agreed to drive her to work and collect her in the evenings. She ought to be safe enough in the salon.

Brenda sat in the car but did not immediately start the engine. The pattern had been broken; broken twice. Janice was not self-employed nor did her salary come into the same bracket as the women she had already seen. And now one of those women was dead.

The salon was unisex. Janice would come into contact

with many men as well as women. Maybe the man they were looking for had had his hair cut there, maybe only once. If so Janice could hardly be expected to remember him. They could always go through the appointments book. In fact, she decided, she would do so now on the off-chance that Smithson had been a customer.

It was a waste of time, the name Smithson was not recorded for any time that year, but he might have used another name. Brenda set off once more. The remaining women must be warned.

Poor Julie Watson, she thought. Although she had met her only once she knew she had had a lot going for her. Divorced, like herself, and, she recalled, like Maggie Telford. She shook her head as she waited for a set of lights to change to green. For a second she had wondered if they had been married to the same man, albeit at different times. Maggie had reverted to her maiden name, she did not know her married one.

Pamela Richards, Cassandra Maguire and Maggie Telford were professional women; Janice was not. But they all came into contact with many people through the course of their work. Maybe Maggie Telford had treated Smithson. They had brought the man in and they had let him go. Yet it was often the first and most obvious solution that was right. He had, after all, been given the oppor-tunity to call Julie during the early hours of Monday morning and then later to kill her, thanks to their having released him.

Short would be dealing with the murder scene. By now the scene-of-crime team should have arrived, along with photographers, all of whom would get to work as soon as the Home Office pathologist had finished examining the body. But what of Jim Hurst who had employed Julie? How many times had the murderer been the one to report the finding of the body?

Speculating was a waste of time. Facts were required and she still had two women to speak to that morning.

Helen Potter and Maggie Telford. Maggie was next on the list.

It was nearer eleven than the ten thirty she had suggested when Brenda pulled into one of the parking spaces allocated for patients of the surgery. The car-park had once been the garden belonging to the large solid, brick-built Victorian house which now accommodated three dentists, their assistants and two hygienists. Typical of its era, there were coloured panes of glass in the front door and a small conservatory to one side.

Brenda pressed the buzzer and was admitted by a mousy-looking girl in a white coat and white leather clogs. There were black and white tiles on the floor of the entry hall but no other traces of the house's origins. The walls had been painted in pastel shades and were adorned with vibrant modern art. But no amount of redecoration could compensate for the smell common to all dental practices. And from behind a closed door came the whine of a drill. Brenda winced. Her teeth were white and even and she went for regular check-ups. Even though she rarely needed more than a scale and polish the anticipation of the visits was always worse than the actual ordeal.

'I've come to see Miss Telford, she's expecting me,' Brenda said as she produced her identity.

'I'll let her know you're here.' The girl disappeared, leaving Brenda standing in the hallway. Perhaps she didn't like the police, a patient would have been shown into the waiting-room. Within seconds Maggie Telford appeared, an apprehensive smile on her face.

'This way,' she said, leading Brenda to a door at the back of the building before she had a chance to apologize for being late. 'I'm between clients but my next one's due in at quarter past.'

They entered a sitting-room which held five armchairs, a coffee table, a shelf bearing books relating to dentistry and another table upon which was a filter coffee machine with two hotplates. One jug was full, the other held an inch or so of murky liquid. The staff must have a caffeine addiction.

Without asking, Maggie filled two mugs from the full jug and handed one to Brenda. 'Help yourself to milk and sugar.'

'Black's fine, thanks.' Brenda sat down wondering why Miss Telford was finding it difficult to meet her eyes. She, too, was dressed in white and a green mask hung around her neck. Her dark, lustrous hair was wound into a neat coil at the back of her head. 'What is it you wanted to see me about?' There was a hint of belligerence in her voice.

'About the calls you've been receiving.'

'I've explained all that, and you got him, didn't you?'

'Mr Smithson admitted making telephone calls to your number, but he firmly denies contacting the other women.'

'Fair enough, maybe someone else made those. Look, I hope he knows he can't get away with it. Have you charged him?'

'No.'

'Why ever not? He's admitted it.'

'It isn't that simple, Miss Telford. Mr Smithson insists that he knows you, that you went out together and that you knew perfectly well it was him who was calling.'

'Then he's a liar.'

Stalemate, Brenda thought. Someone is lying, but who? 'And there's been a development.' She explained about the similarities between the women then paused before adding, 'And one of them has been murdered.'

'What?' Maggie's hazel eyes widened in shock. 'Are you suggesting that this man, this pervert you've released back on to the streets is now going to kill us all?'

How could she answer? It was always a possibility. 'I came here to warn you. We will, of course, be doing all we can to protect you.'

'Twenty-four hours a day?' Brenda said nothing. 'No, I thought not.'

'You mentioned you thought you were being watched.'

'Yes.' Once again she looked away. Two spots of colour had come into her face. 'But it was just a feeling, I might've been wrong.'

Now there's a chance of real danger she's backing off. I wonder why? Brenda asked herself. She requested a list of people known to her. Maggie said she would provide one. 'May I also have a list of your patients?'

'Of course.' Maggie stood, relieved that the interview was at an end. 'There's no Smithson, not on any of our lists. I've already checked.'

Within minutes the computer printer had disgorged several sheets of paper. Patients' names were listed alphabetically under the name of each of the dentists. Maggie's two partners were both male. It would probably be necessary to speak to them at some point.

Brenda left with a sense of unease. Something was wrong. She was convinced that Maggie Telford had been lying, if only by omission. Once she had spoken to Helen Potter she would try to make some sense of it all. But as she drove her mind was on Julie Watson. A good-looking intelligent woman who had been on the verge of starting a new life had now had that chance taken away from her.

'We're in luck,' John Short said to Alan Campbell as they waited for the pathologist to finish his examination. 'The scene hasn't been contaminated.' Jim Hurst had not entered the kitchen, only stood in the doorway. The point of access for the killer had been the kitchen door, which opened inwards from the back of the building. They had found it closed but unlocked. And the place was spotless, had never been cooked in. And they had two days to finish their forensic examination without interruption as the opening wasn't until Friday night, if it went ahead as planned. 'Go and see how he is.' Short nodded in the

41

direction of Hurst's office. He had, he said, remained there ever since he had made the call.

Alan Campbell, thin and pale, sandy-haired and with pale blue eyes, had never lost his Scottish accent. He appeared undernourished, ill almost, but was neither of those things, it was simply the way he was made, a legacy of his puritanical father's genes. Once married, he now eschewed women. He had adored his wife, put her on a pedestal, only to discover that her naked beauty was not for his eyes only. She had been appearing in pornographic films throughout the length of their marriage. For this he would never forgive her nor would he ever trust another female. Yet he did not allow this to cloud his vision where work was concerned. Not for a minute did he think that these six women had done something to deserve receiving obscene telephone calls. And Julie Watson had died, had been stabbed in the back, the act of a coward as well as a murderer.

He rapped quietly on the office door and heard a faint 'Come in.' Jim Hurst was deathly white. He sat behind his desk with a half-filled tumbler of brandy in front of him. He took a small sip. 'I wouldn't normally drink this early,' he said as if he needed to excuse himself. 'It was such a shock, she was a lovely person.'

Alan sat opposite him. 'Did you know her well?'

'Not socially. I needed a kitchen designer. I'd contacted several and interviewed them. She was the one with the best ideas so therefore she was the one I chose. Our relationship was strictly business.'

'How long ago was the interview?'

'About six months. We only ever met here but she was always pleasant and cheerful and she certainly knew what she was doing.'

'And lately, was she still cheerful?'

Jim Hurst turned the glass between both of his hands. He frowned. 'She was a little preoccupied the last time I saw her.' He stopped and took another sip of the brandy.

'The last time I saw her alive. She said she was coming in yesterday to check the final deliveries.'

'Did she give a time?'

'No.'

'Did she mention any phone calls?'

'No. We only talked about the job. Why?'

'It's not important.' Alan did not think this badly shaken man was the murderer but he might be a brilliant actor. They would, of course, look into his background. 'Do you know any of these women?' He handed him a sheet of paper on which were written five names.

Jim Hurst looked up and met Alan's eyes. 'Yes. Well, not know exactly, know of. Maggie Telford.'

Alan, fully alert, nodded. Would he have admitted it if he was guilty? 'How do you know her?'

'She's a partner at the dental practice I use. My dentist's Phillip Jackson, but her name's on the plaque outside and I've seen her once or twice although I've never spoken to her.'

Brenda might know this already. She was seeing Miss Telford and would have requested a list of patients. And if Hurst was guilty of making those calls he would realize this and know that he could not deny the connection, however tenuous. 'Any of the others?'

'Sorry, no.'

'Okay, what can you tell us about Julie Watson?'

It appeared to be very little. Hurst knew nothing of her private life, they had only discussed the restaurant.

'What about this? What do I do about it?' He slid the invoice to Alan's side of the desk.

'Nothing for the moment. The cheque will go into her estate, but it might be best to wait until we've contacted the next-of-kin.' There would probably be an accountant to sort out her financial matters. Despite self-assessment for tax purposes most self-employed people still used professional help.

Alan stood up. 'That's it for now, but we might need to speak to you again.'

Jim Hurst nodded as he picked up his glass. He seemed genuinely shocked and upset.

Once the team had finished in the kitchen they'd have access to the contents of Julie Watson's handbag. Then they might learn a little more about the woman who lay dead on the floor.

Chapter Four

On Wednesday morning Matthew Watson was in a board meeting when a secretary interrupted it to say there was an urgent telephone call for him. He excused himself, cursing the disturbance because he had almost succeeded in swinging the majority of voters to his way of thinking. The supermarket chain of which he was area manager was making a profit but competition was fierce, price wars were doing them no favours. He wanted more loss leaders on basic food items but there was pressure from every direction. Farmers had blockaded deliveries of milk to supermarkets because they were losing money. Identifying with their situation, he had suggested they pay the suppliers a few pence more but sell it at cost price to keep the customers happy as well. To compensate they could add five, or even ten pence on items such as tinned anchovies or pickled walnuts and other luxury goods where the increase would not be as noticeable to customers who expected such products to be expensive.

'Yes?' His manner was terse as he took the call. Watching him, the girl at the switchboard noticed the change in his body language. No longer the high-powered executive, Matthew Watson's shoulders slumped. 'I see,' he said. 'Yes, I'll be here for the rest of the morning.' He hung up and returned to the meeting not knowing what lay ahead, only that the police wanted to speak to him and that it sounded like bad news.

Half an hour later, despite the brief disruption, the board voted in favour of Matthew's proposals. Gathering their papers, the twelve members began to converse on other subjects. No one seemed to have noticed Matthew's changed demeanour.

The regional administration offices of the supermarket chain for which Matthew worked were situated on three floors of one of the new buildings near the town hall. When the board of directors learned that that area of the town was to be regenerated they had decided to transfer their headquarters from Ipswich to Rickenham Green, and, of course, the rents were cheaper. Matthew, who lived in the town, had been pleased. It meant he had less travelling to do.

The success of the meeting palled as he waited for the police, watching his coffee grow cold.

It was almost two when his secretary knocked on the door. 'Detective Sergeant Grant and Constable Prance to see you, sir,' she said, closing the door behind her.

Gregory Grant looked a little less drawn than when Brenda had spoken to him on Monday evening. He was sleeping well in the new house and he had been made to feel welcome by his new colleagues. Tragic as it was, a murder inquiry would take his mind off his own grief.

'Mr Watson, as I said on the phone, we have some bad news.' How else could you put it? There could not have been anyone who did not realize what those words prefaced. Greg paused for a couple of seconds to let the inadequate sentence sink in. 'Your ex-wife has been found dead and we need an official identification. If you'd prefer not to be the one to do this we'd be grateful if you could let us have the name of her parents or siblings or whoever she now lists as her next-of-kin.'

Matthew nodded and stared at his hands which were clasped on the desk in front of him. 'I'll do it. She doesn't have any brothers or sisters and her parents live in Portugal. There's nobody else apart from a senile grandmother. Do you want me to come now?'

'No, sometime later this afternoon, if that's convenient for you.' The time the forensic team took to go over the

46

scene of a crime varied. In this instance there seemed no doubt that Julie Watson had been killed where she lay. Even to DC Campbell who had contacted base with the preliminary findings it was obvious that the pooling of blood was consistent with her having been stabbed in that brand new kitchen. Ironical that the place she had designed with such care had become the place of her death. 'Say five, five thirty?'

'I'll be there.' He frowned. 'Where, though? Do I come to the police station?' This was only a couple of minutes' walk from his own office.

'No. A car will pick you up here. We'll drive you to the hospital mortuary.' Rickenham General was a huge complex on the outskirts of the town. Once, there had been several small hospitals within walking distance of the High Street; now they no longer existed. Anyone requiring Accident and Emergency, admission or an outpatient's appointment had to travel a fair distance for treatment. Bigger, Greg decided, was not always better. How did pensioners manage, and pregnant women with another small child? He shook his head imperceptibly. It was best not to think about hospitals. He had spent most of the last year of his wife's life visiting her in one. 'Is there anything you'd like to ask us?'

'No.' Matthew shook his head, wondering at his own stupidity. 'Yes. Yes, there is. How did she die? It was an accident, I take it?'

'No, it wasn't an accident, sir.'

Matthew was stunned. For some reason he had imagined she had fallen from a ladder or sustained injuries whilst on a building site. Occasionally she was involved in the initial layout of a building. She hadn't been ill, he would have known. They had kept in touch, not frequently, but she would have told him if that was the case. She would never have killed herself so there was only one other alternative. He had to know. 'Are you trying to say she was murdered?'

'We are treating it as murder, sir.' Not that there was any

47

doubt. Julie Watson had not stabbed herself in the back, but phrasing it that way might help to soften the impact. Greg felt hot in the stuffy room. There were no windows open and the large expanse of glass created a greenhouse effect. No air seemed to come through the slotted vents at the top. 'We'll need to ask you some questions when you're up to it.'

Matthew nodded. He had expected as much.

Just as he was about to leave, Greg realized what he had done. The circumstances were different, that was all. He had been the bearer of bad news. Only last year a doctor had broken the same news to him, but in Greg's case he had loved his wife, had still been married to her. He had known how ill she was but he would never, ever forgive himself for not being there at the end. It had come suddenly, days before the medical staff had expected it. He had not had a chance to say goodbye. But neither had Matthew Watson. He might have been divorced but that didn't mean he had no feelings for Julie. On the other hand, he might have killed her. Greg felt his spirits lift. That was more like it, he needed to think rationally, not like the man he had been in danger of becoming before his transfer: a cipher, nothing more.

They knew there had been a third party involved in the divorce because Julie had explained her circumstances to Brenda after she reported the first telephone call. 'I'm divorced now, I live alone,' she had said. 'My husband left me for another woman.' But Julie may have been making demands upon Matthew, may have started making his life a misery. Some abandoned women were like that. Some women refused to let go even when the ex-spouse had a new family, so, whatever he claimed, maybe Matthew Watson did have a reason to wish her dead. Later would come the questions. First they had to make certain that the woman really was Julie Watson. They had Jim Hurst's say-so and the contents of her handbag to prove it but an official identification was required.

Six women, he thought, six women who live alone and

look alike. All had received unwelcome telephone calls on various dates either during the late evening or in the early hours of the morning. And one of them was dead. Were the rest in danger? Could they be protected? Or was the murder unrelated? It was a possibility but only a slim one. There was some element which connected these women that had placed their lives in danger. But would they find it in time?

DS Grant returned to the station. Brenda Gibbons should have returned with the information she had gleaned from Janice King, Maggie Telford and Helen Potter. Pamela Richards and Cassandra Maguire would also know the score by now. Greg prayed that the women were not too independent to heed the warning. I never thought it would happen to me, was all too often the victim's cry.

The afternoon passed slowly for Matthew. He might have reached his mid-thirties but he had never witnessed death before. His own parents were relatively young and all his grandparents were still alive. If it really was Julie, and he kept trying to convince himself that the police had made a mistake, how would he feel when he saw her? They had lived together for seven years, shared meals and a bed and friends. Yes, he still felt something for her and maybe the old adage about the seven-year itch was true. Even now he wasn't sure exactly what had gone wrong other than that the marriage had become stale. Admit it, he told himself, it wasn't so much that as the fact that Debbie flattered my ego and I fell for it. He had been with Debbie for nearly two years now and was beginning to see that the age difference might be a problem in the long term. She was twenty-two and had different expectations from life than himself. He wondered how ageing film stars did it, took up with someone young enough to be their granddaughter, but, presumably, money was a big factor. Accepted, it was nice to be seen out with Debbie who was slender and sexy and clearly young, but would that be enough in years to come? And she clearly wanted children whereas he wasn't bothered. I should've stayed with Julie, I should've tried to make a go of it, he thought.

'Stop it,' he muttered. 'Stop it right there.' He knew he was trying to blame himself in some way, that the if onlys would haunt him for some time. If they were still married would Julie have been wherever she was at the time she was killed? I didn't ask, he realized, I have no idea where or when or how she was murdered. For his own peace of mind he intended to find out.

It was a little after five when a different officer appeared to drive him to the mortuary.

'Yes, that's Julie.' Matthew shivered. After the warmth of the sun it was cold in the building. He felt oddly relieved. Now he had seen her he could start believing she was dead; but it was more than that, she had looked almost peaceful, as if she was asleep. There were no horrible injuries that he could see but her body had been covered with a sheet.

'Are you all right?' the officer asked.

'Yes, thanks. Just a bit shaken.'

'Are you up to answering a few questions at the station?'

Matthew nodded. He had had all afternoon to think about it and knew they would not wait long to interview him. Naturally he would be a suspect, they looked closest to home first. Idly, he wondered if he had an alibi.

He was driven back to the town centre and escorted into an interview room. He felt mentally exhausted but ready to help if he could. Only when he was introduced to Detective Chief Inspector Roper did he realize how tenuous his position was. He had expected someone of lesser rank to interview him, but he was not aware of Ian's methods of working. He liked to know the people involved, by speaking to them, not by reading reports or listening to tapes. So much more could be gained from watching a suspect or witness.

'To be able to solve this crime we need to know as much

as possible about your ex-wife,' Ian began once the formalities were over. 'Anything you can tell us might be of help.'

'Where would you like me to start?'

'From the time you first met.' DS Grant had informed Ian that Julie Watson's parents were living abroad. The Portuguese police should have spoken to them by now. Her paternal grandmother was in a home suffering from Alzheimer's disease but would still be informed of the death by the nursing staff even if she was unable to understand what had happened.

The way in which they had met was probably one of the most conventional, as was the way the relationship had developed. He and Julie had been introduced at a party. After seeing each other for almost a year they had lived together, then married.

'I'd just got promotion to area general manager, it was the ideal time to marry and buy a house. Julie had a degree in art and design but she wasn't established then. Over the years she did a few jobs to keep her hand in. When I left she started full time. But money was never a problem between us.'

'So what went wrong?' Ian, already knowing the answer, studied the man across the table. He was handsome in a boyish way, smartly dressed in a lightweight suit, articulate and willing to co-operate. But there was a slackness about his mouth suggesting a touch of hedonism, which was probably why he had been led astray. He wore a plain gold ring on his right hand, possibly his wedding ring which had been transferred after the divorce.

'We'd been married about seven years when I met someone else,' he answered honestly and without elaboration. 'The usual story, I'm afraid. We met through work. Debbie works for the accounts department.'

'Were there problems over the divorce?'

'Not really. I knew Julie was devastated but she didn't let it show. She always held her emotions in check, that was her way. Maybe it had something to do with her brother.'

'Her brother?' Ian leaned forward. He did not turn to DS Grant who sat beside him and who had reported that Watson had told him there were no siblings.

'He died when he was four and Julie was nine. She rarely talked about him but I don't think she ever got over it. God, her poor parents . . .' He did not complete the sentence but there was no need. To lose two children was unthinkable.

'After you separated, what happened?'

'Once I'd told Julie there was someone else I moved out almost immediately. It wouldn't have been fair to her to stay with her knowing that whilst I was out I was seeing Debbie. I got some temporary accommodation until we found somewhere together. I made sure Julie was looked after financially. She bought the house in Maple Grove with what I gave her as a settlement although she had to put some of her own money towards it.'

'You didn't split everything fifty-fifty?'

'No. It's what my solicitor suggested but neither of us knew how secure Julie's business was and I felt guilty enough as it was. Conscience money, I suppose you could call it. Give her her due, she never asked me for another penny.'

Julie hadn't been a drain on his finances so money was not the motive. They would check this, naturally. 'Did you keep in touch?'

'Yes. There was no need to really, but I liked to make sure she was all right. It'll sound ridiculous to you, considering the circumstances, but there were times when I missed her. I'll miss her more than ever now.'

Regrets, Ian thought. Watson hadn't made it through the bad patch which ended many marriages. Had he stuck it out he might have been happy. Perhaps he would feel the same about Debbie a few years hence. 'Did your ex-wife contact you often? For instance, was she the sort of woman

52

who constantly needed things mending around the house?'

Matthew smiled. 'Definitely not. There were few things she couldn't do herself and she never intruded upon my relationship with Debbie. We remained friends, spoke on the phone occasionally, but that's all.'

'Did you ever suspect there might have been another man in her life, either during your marriage or afterwards?'

'No. I would be willing to swear that she was faithful.' He paused. 'But maybe all men think that.'

'Did she mention any obscene telephone calls?'

'Good heavens, no. Why?'

'She had received some during the weeks preceding her death.'

'And you think the same man is responsible for killing her? Hold on, didn't I read something about that in the *Herald*?'

'Yes. Your ex-wife was one of those women.'

'I see. I didn't know. I wish she'd told me.'

The dejection was genuine, the man seemed to still care for Julie Watson. He looked hesitantly at Ian. 'May I ask you a question?'

'Of course.'

'Two, in fact. How and where did she die?'

Ian sat back and folded his arms. It had not yet been decided how much to tell the press. A statement would be made which would appear in the weekly edition of the *Rickenham Herald* on Friday. The relatives had been informed, so the victim could be named. There seemed no harm in telling the man. If he was guilty he would know anyway. 'She was working on that new restaurant, La Pêche – her body was found there, in the kitchen. She had been stabbed.'

'Oh, Christ.' Matthew put his head in his hands. 'Did she – would she have suffered?'

It was a question that was almost always asked, one to which there was no honest answer. How could anyone know? 'We think not.' If it was a lie it was a well-intentioned one. They would not know until after the post-mortem in the morning if the first of the two blows had killed her, and maybe not then.

Tea was brought in and for the next half-hour Matthew told them all he could about the woman he had married.

'What did you think?' Ian asked Greg when Matthew Watson had been advised that he was free to leave.

'I think he was telling the truth. And I think she would've recognized his voice if it was him making those calls.'

'Maybe.' Ian thought over what they had learned. Julie loved her job, did her own housework, cooking and minor repairs, swam at the municipal baths occasionally and played tennis in the summer if she could find a partner. Matthew had never played. But she used the public courts. It seemed few people visited the house.

'She wasn't a joiner,' Matthew had said. 'She disliked the idea of having to be in the same place at the same time once a week or whatever. She was very much a spur of the moment person.'

'No regular routine, sir,' Greg commented as if he had read Ian's thoughts. 'That makes it harder for us.'

'But someone got hold of her phone number and someone killed her. Her back was turned. Either she trusted this person completely or he took her totally by surprise.'

'I think it was the former, I think she must have known him.'

They were heading towards the canteen. Greg pushed open the swing door and held it for Ian.

'What makes you say that?'

'She was frightened enough of those calls to contact us. The third time she said she had the feeling that someone was watching her. With all that on her mind surely she wouldn't have gone into an empty building in a pretty isolated spot and left the door unlocked. That's the only way she could have been taken by surprise. There was no forced entry. Maybe he was already with her, maybe she let him in after she arrived there believing herself to be safe. Who more likely than her ex-husband?'

Ian nodded as he headed towards the counter. And maybe Watson had lied to them, maybe he hadn't wanted to leave but Julie had thrown him out, maybe he decided to take it out on all the dark-haired females he had somehow met. And what better place than a supermarket? Okay, he worked in the head office of the chain but he would have to visit the consumer outlets to keep in touch and up to date.

It was now Wednesday. No one had reported another call since Monday night. Julie had been the one to receive it. Had the caller tired of being anonymous and moved on to bigger things? 'We'll have a quick coffee, see what Brenda has to say, and then we'll listen to Smithson's tape,' Ian decided as he wondered what time he would make it home.

DS Grant was surprised when the Chief paid for their drinks. He was beginning to think he would enjoy working in his new division.

Ian glanced at the large clock on the wall. He had better ring Moira to let her know he'd be late. There would be no decorating done that evening, possibly not for some time to come.

Chapter Five

At ten to seven on Wednesday evening the members of
Ian's team were gathered in the general office. Coffee and
plastic-wrapped sandwiches sat on one of the desks. Ian
had run through the basics of the interview with Matthew
Watson, it was now up to the rest of them to find out
everything and anything about his ex-wife and everyone
she had come into contact with. 'What did you make of
Hurst?' he asked DC Alan Campbell.

'Would you like to listen to the tapes, sir?'

'No, I'd rather you told me what you thought first.'

'He hasn't given us much to go on. If what he says is
true then he didn't know her socially and they'd never met
other than at the restaurant. He went there this morning,
saw her car, assumed she was making her final check a day
late then found the body in the kitchen. He was in quite a
state.'

As he would be had he killed her, was the general, silent
consensus.

'We'll come back to him later. Naturally we'll speak to
him again but we'll get some background first. See if you
can confirm his movements from Tuesday onwards.' Hurst
might have had a motive, sexual perhaps, or financial if he
couldn't afford to pay Julie's bill. Alan had mentioned the
cheque but Hurst might have written it after he had killed
her. 'Brenda, let's hear how you got on.'

DC Brenda Gibbons sat on the edge of a desk, her slim
legs swinging. She was aware of Short's eyes on her san-
dalled feet and painted nails and wondered if, amongst his

other revolting habits, he might also be a foot fetishist. She could smell his sweat from where she sat. 'Pamela Richards and Cassandra Maguire are either conscientious or more frightened than they're admitting. They both dropped their lists in first thing this morning. The name Smithson isn't on either of them and none of the names they provided appear on both lists. The only thing they have in common is membership of the new gym attached to the squash club. They both joined when it first opened because they were offering reduced rates for the first year. Pam's only used it three times, Cassandra goes more regularly. But as they haven't named each other presumably they've never met, or, if they have, they don't realize it.'

'And the other lovely ladies?' Short sprayed spittle as he spoke. He was chewing a fingernail. He stopped nibbling to leer as Brenda recrossed her legs. Tonight he had arranged to see Nancy of the ample thighs and heaving bosom. He would have been mortified to learn that he thought in terms more relevant to a romantic novelist than a detective inspector.

'The other lovely ladies are also terrified,' Brenda replied pointedly. Couldn't the man even take murder seriously? His licentiousness overruled his emotions. 'Janice King will be staying with her brother and his wife, Helen Potter's going to her sister, who's also her business partner, and Maggie Telford implied she didn't trust us and would make whatever arrangements she thought suitable, not that she enlightened me as to what they were.'

'And those three are working on their lists?'

'Yes, sir. But I've already got a print-out of Maggie Telford's dental clients.'

Ian had half-heartedly hoped that Miss Telford would prove to be the link, that the other women had been patients, as he preferred to call them, at the surgery. 'And there's nothing to connect them so far?'

'Not yet.' Not apart from the length and colour of their hair, Brenda thought. And Janice King was a hairdresser. But she had checked the appointments book; it wasn't only

Smithson's name which had not been in evidence, none of the women's names had appeared either. Brenda realized that the back-street salon was not the sort of place likely to be patronized by Pamela Richards, Cass Maguire or Maggie Telford.

'Sir, you said we'd get back to Jim Hurst.'

Ian, who was debating whether or not to spoil his dinner by opening one of the packets of sandwiches, glanced at Alan Campbell. 'Go on.'

'I do have a bit of local background. He's a patient at the dental surgery where Maggie Telford works. Not one of Miss Telford's, though. The man he sees is called Phillip Jackson. Hurst claims not to have spoken to Miss Telford but he recognized the name and admits to having seen her there on a couple of occasions.'

Brenda bit her lip. She had studied Maggie's client list thoroughly but had not had time for more than a quick look at those of the other partners. On the other hand, she had not known until her return that afternoon that the name of the owner of La Pêche was Jim Hurst.

'This sounds more like it. Hurst employed Julie Watson, maybe he knew her more intimately than he's letting on, and he has had contact, however minimal, with Maggie. I wonder how well he knows the others.'

'He says he doesn't.'

Short took a slurp of cooling coffee. On his desk lay a half-eaten sandwich; a protruding piece of ham was already starting to curl in the evening sunlight which now, late in the day, slanted through the blinds on the opposite side of the room. Short's plump thighs were spread, straining the seams of his trousers and hiding the seat of his chair. 'And what did our Mr Hurst do before he bought the restaurant?' He looked at Alan who had also questioned him informally initially.

'He had another restaurant, in the Lake District. He made a lot of money from the business and sold the place at a good profit.'

'And decided that Rickenham Green, Mecca of East Anglia, was the ideal spot to start again?'

Alan glowered at Short. 'Yes. He got tired of the tourist trade, of people not appreciating the sort of meals he wanted to serve. He said he'd had to include chips on the menu and that half of the customers shovelled their food down so fast they couldn't possibly have tasted it. He saw the ad in a trade journal and made an offer which was accepted.'

'A food snob. And he thinks we citizens of Rickenham Green will fall over ourselves in the rush to get to La Pêche for a spot of coulis or a drizzle of passion fruit jus?'

Several pairs of eyes met across the room. Brenda hid a barely disguised smile. That Scruffy Short, connoisseur of junk food and bacon and brown sauce sandwiches, had ever even heard such words came as a total surprise.

'Do we know anything else about him?' DS Grant longed to be part of the group. He still felt on the fringes although it was early days yet, but he had spent some time observing his colleagues. To an outsider it might seem that Brenda Gibbons and John Short were enemies but despite their disparate looks, manners and behaviour it was apparent that there was mutual respect. And Alan Campbell, what a dour, humourless man he appeared to be but there was more to him than that. Beneath the surface was a strong sense of morality tempered with compassion. Greg wondered if, like himself, Alan had suffered some personal tragedy.

'Sorry I'm late.' The door crashed open. Detective Constable Eddie Roberts looked vaguely embarrassed at his mistimed, noisy entrance. 'It's taken the whole damn day to tie up the paperwork. There seems to be more with every new case.'

They all knew that Eddie had been involved in a case of systematic car thefts; cars stolen on demand for pre-ordained customers, not nicked, driven away then set alight by kids out for a laugh.

Brenda's mind was elsewhere as Ian outlined the facts

for Eddie. As feminist as some of her views were, it only struck her then that she was the only female on the team. Her life had been hard but she had made it and was doing a job she loved. Alan had also come through a crisis and she would bet money that so had Greg. The Chief, moody as he could be at times, led a stable existence. He loved his wife, not that he ever said so, but it was obvious by the way in which he spoke of Moira. Eddie Roberts was transparent. Like a big, soft labrador, was how Brenda thought of him. Brown eyes, floppy brown hair, happily married with two small children and a house that was always full of relatives from one or other side of the family. And he loved it. That left Scruffy Short. Brenda suppressed a sigh of exasperation. Short was Short and that was that. A lecher of the first degree. That anyone could fancy him was beyond belief. She took in the roll of flesh hiding his belt, his threadbare jacket, stained shirt and scuffed shoes and shuddered. Perhaps the luxuriant if straggling moustache had been grown to compensate for the bald pate over which a few strands of hair were brushed. Their origins lay somewhere behind his left ear. But there was a woman. A female PC had seen Short with her. 'Red-headed and blowsy' was how she had described her.

Brenda felt tired, but it was no excuse for forgetfulness. Alan was not the only one to have made a connection. 'I should've mentioned it, sir,' she began once Eddie Roberts had been brought up to date. 'Pamela Richards listed Doc Harris as her GP.'

A couple of seconds of silence followed this remark. Doc Harris was a local, old-fashioned GP who was also on the rota of police surgeons and a good friend of the Chief's.

'The Doc?' Short laughed. 'Well, stranger things have happened at sea.'

Eddie Roberts groaned. Clichés were bad enough, the least the man could do was to quote them accurately.

'I'll speak to him. Remind me, Pamela Richards is . . .?'

'The window-dresser. She lives in a cottage out near Little Endesley.'

'Thanks.' With six women involved the names were confusing but within the next couple of days that would no longer be the case. He would know them as well as he knew those of his colleagues. Ian picked up the phone. Doc Harris was still in surgery but he took the call when he knew who was ringing. He agreed to meet Ian at nine o'clock in the Crown. Better there than the Elms Golf and Country Club where the Doc was a member and where there was a distinct danger of imbibing too many single-malt whiskies. Ian could walk home from the Crown. He hung up, allowing Jim Harris to believe it was to be a social meeting.

'And now for Anthony Smithson, then we'll all go home.' Smithson had been picked up earlier at the insurance offices where he worked.

Ian placed a tape into the recorder which stood on an unused desk and switched it on. They listened to DS Gregory Grant introduce himself and name the others present. Then he gave the date and time. He had been the one to interview Smithson when he'd returned from breaking the news to Julie's ex-husband, Matthew Watson.

'We've had to bring you back because we need to be certain of our facts, we need to double-check a couple of things,' Grant had begun.

'Of course. That's quite all right.' Smithson sounded calm, almost relaxed.

'You're a member of the claims department at A.G. & S. Insurance, is that right?'

'Yes, I am.'

'And you're in the process of buying your own flat.'

'That's right, but you know all this already and I don't see why it' s relevant.'

But those listening did. Gregory Grant was not inexperienced, he knew exactly what he was doing. Repetitive questions could rattle a suspect, make him lose his temper and give away more than he had intended. As Brenda had commented, he was not a loser or unemployed and bored or a mummy's boy. He seemed to have quite a lot going for him.

'You've admitted you rang Maggie Telford on Monday evening. Why from a call box?'

'Do I really have to go through all this again? I've already answered your questions. You have a record of my answers on tape. Wouldn't it be easier for you to listen to it again?'

'We'd prefer to hear it in your own words again.'

He sighed audibly. 'All right. I was supposed to be meeting a friend for a drink. He didn't turn up. I don't particularly like Bank Holidays and I was at a loose end. As I was already in the town centre I thought I'd try Maggie and see if she was free. She'd said she didn't want to see me again but she hadn't had a chance to get to know me. I thought it was worth one more try.'

Ian stopped the tape, rewound it a little and played the last few sentences over again. He had not met Smithson, had not been present to assess his body language but he certainly came across as if he had nothing to hide, as if he really had known Maggie. Just the right amount of frustration and anger at being questioned again, just enough peevishness for a man who felt he was being unjustly treated. Ian let the tape play on.

'One more try?' Grant had asked.

'Look, I've said all this before although it's obvious no one believes me, but I'd taken her out a couple of times. Well, twice, in fact. I liked her a lot, she's the sort of person I admire. I thought she was exactly the sort of woman I needed. Someone strong and independent. I was wrong. She can't have liked me much at all to do as she has done.'

Needed? Did the use of that particular word smack of obsession? Ian wondered.

'She denies knowing you.'

'I don't know why. She gave me the brush-off. She didn't exactly tell me so at first, she just kept saying she was too busy to see me whenever I rang. And now this.' He paused. 'All right, I rang her several times over the past couple of weeks. I suppose she came to see me as a nuisance. I wanted to let her know how I felt but she wouldn't give me the chance.'

Ian thought this did sound obsessional, especially if he'd only seen her once or twice.

'I thought we were getting on really well. She seemed interested. Like I said, I got it wrong.'

'I understand you've had other relationships in the past. Were the women all dark-haired?'

'No. Some, but not all.' Smithson sounded puzzled.

'You've never married?'

'No. But there's plenty of time, I'm only thirty.' He paused again. 'I nearly did once.'

'What went wrong?'

'She decided she wasn't ready for marriage, at least, not to me.'

'How did you react to that?'

'I was hurt and angry, naturally. Then I realized that I was exaggerating those feelings, that they were things I thought I was supposed to feel. After a month or so I stopped missing her and felt only relief. By then I'd realized the marriage would never have worked.'

'Her name?'

'Whatever do you need it for?'

'Her name, please, Mr Smithson.'

'Isobel French. She's married now, her maiden name was Evans. I heard she's moved away from Rickenham Green but I don't know where she lives now.'

'Thank you. Where were you on Tuesday night, from between five thirty and the time you arrived at work this morning?'

Discreet inquiries had ascertained that Smithson had arrived at work at eight fifty that day, having parked his car in the company's car-park. The enormous building that housed the insurance offices was on the outskirts of the town.

Smithson sighed. 'I left work at about quarter to six. I took a long call from one of the solicitors who deals with our defendant claims so I was running late. I drove straight to the squash club where I'd booked a court for six. My partner was already waiting. We played for an hour, showered and changed and had a drink.

'I left around seven thirty, picked up an Indian takeaway and went home. I'd videoed something I wanted to watch.'

'Did you pay for the food with a credit card?'

'No, cash.'

'Did you go out again at any time?'

'No.'

His movements until he left the squash club could be verified easily but unless he was a regular at the takeaway it was unlikely the people who ran it would remember him, and there were all those other hours to account for. 'Would any of your neighbours have heard you come in?'

'I've no idea.'

But like Brenda after the first interview with Smithson, Ian couldn't decide if what he was hearing was true. Innocent people were rarely able to supply an adequate alibi because they did not know they needed one. Not that they knew exactly when Julie Watson had been killed, only that it was after the time Jim Hurst had said he left the restaurant on Tuesday morning and before he found her on Wednesday morning. Unless Hurst had returned to kill her and, in the way of others before him, then gone back to the scene to report the crime.

'Notice anything?' Short said to the room in general as he tugged at his moustache.

'The squash club. Both Pamela Richards and Cass Maguire use, or have used, the gym there,' Greg Grant said immediately.

'Quite. Hopefully we haven't let a murderer go twice.' Short sounded almost unconcerned.

'What did Helen Potter have to say, Brenda?' She did not

64

like to remind Ian that he'd said they could all go after listening to the Smithson tape.

Brenda recalled what had happened that morning. She had left the car in the police station car-park and crossed the road at the pedestrian lights. A warm breeze had stirred her hair. Already the streets were dusty as if summer was almost over and not about to begin. Ahead of her lay the well-patronized sandwich bar which served the staff of the town hall, council offices and other municipal buildings which had been erected around three sides of a paved area in which the saplings were finally starting to mature and where the statue of a local dignitary was already covered with pigeon droppings. In the centre was a small fountain which sprayed passers-by if the wind blew strongly. None of these additions saved the buildings, including the police station adjacent to them, from ugliness.

Wise move, Brenda had thought as she pushed open the sandwich bar door. Helen Potter and her sister had chosen a prime location when they had decided to open the place as a joint venture. The High Street was a ten-minute walk away, the majority of office workers would sooner simply cross the road as she had done. The parade of shops was relatively new, erected at the same time as the premises opposite. They comprised eight or nine small units with living accommodation over the top. There was a florist, a baker's, a dry-cleaner's, a gift shop, a shoe-repairer's, a newsagent's and one empty unit. The sandwich bar was in the middle.

It was not quite twelve o'clock but already half a dozen people waited to be served. Brenda's mouth had watered at the array of bowls containing salad and sandwich fillings. Behind the counter was a display of breads and rolls. She could smell egg mayonnaise and tuna and warm bread. The two women serving were piling the fillings into open baps with a deftness born of practice. The short, cheerful woman with her dark hair mainly concealed beneath a cap had to be Helen Potter. If the other woman was her sister they looked nothing alike.

Brenda stayed at the front of the shop. Only two customers remained but the door opened and a young woman came in closely followed by two men. They would be rushed off their feet by one o'clock, she would have to act soon.

Now she related only an outline of the interview, the details she kept to herself. As she spoke she tried to recall her impressions of Helen, hoping that she hadn't missed anything which might be relevant.

'Can I help you?' The older, ginger-haired woman had looked at Brenda suspiciously, unaware of her reasons for not inserting herself into the queue.

'I can see you're busy but I'm here to see Helen Potter.'

'Oh, yes. I'm sorry. I should've realized. Helen?' She turned to where her sister was taking change from the till. 'It's the police.'

'Can you cope for a few minutes, Jill?'

'Of course I can. You carry on.' The two women smiled.

'I didn't see you there,' Helen said as she lifted the flap at the side of the counter to allow Brenda entry. 'We've been so busy. In between serving we've been making up trays of sandwiches for some big do over at the town hall. Anyway, they've been collected now. Come on through.'

Brenda ducked beneath Helen's arm as she held up the flap. There wasn't much space behind the counter and only a tiny room at the back with a washroom leading off it. 'We've interviewed a man in connection with those phone calls,' Brenda began.

'Oh, good.' Helen adjusted a hair clip which held her white cap in place.

'Maybe not. We're not sure he's the man we're looking for.' Briefly she explained what had happened without mentioning Julie Watson by name.

'Oh, God. You think – I mean, well, are you saying my

66

life is in danger?' Helen stepped backwards and almost fell into the only chair in the room.

'We don't know. The two things might not be connected but for the moment we're treating them as if they are. We felt it was best to warn you.'

Helen nodded. Her face was pale but she remained calm. 'I can stay here with my sister and her husband. My boyfriend's still away.'

Brenda was aware of her long-term relationship but the man in question had been out of the country for six weeks and was not due to return for another two. 'Is that your sister, in the shop?'

'Yes, that's Jill. They've got a spare bedroom, there won't be a problem. I'll get some things and stay here tonight.'

Brenda made a note of the telephone number. Like the other women involved, Helen said she would provide a list of everyone she came into contact with on a regular basis. 'What about the customers, most of them come in nearly every day?'

'If you know their names, then include them.'

'We finish about three, sometimes a bit later. I'll do it then and bring it over before we leave.' She smiled wanly. 'I should be safe enough in the police station.'

Not if Scruffy Short sees you, Brenda had thought. No female was safe from his lecherous advances. It was odd that a man who was so revolting should have so much confidence in his attractiveness to women. Brenda had said goodbye and left.

Glancing back through the plate glass door she had seen Helen at the counter serving a customer as if nothing unusual was happening. How different these women's reactions had been.

'Okay, that'll do for tonight,' Ian finally declared. Tomorrow they would go through the contents of Julie Watson's handbag and search her house. Normally that would have happened the same day but they had had other priorities. Julie Watson was dead but there was the safety of five other women to consider, and as Julie had not been murdered at home they were unlikely to find any clues there. Only one small team had been assigned to house-to-house inquiries because there were no houses for at least a mile in either direction from La Pêche. But they had erected a police sign asking motorists to come forward if they had noticed any vehicles in the car-park between Tuesday afternoon and Wednesday morning. Unless Julie had driven her killer there herself he or she would have needed some form of transport. Anthony Smithson, Jim Hurst and Matthew Watson were their immediate suspects. The first two men could each be linked to two of the women, the third was the dead woman's ex-husband. But no one believed it would turn out to be that simple. And from that morning the short life of Julie Watson had become public property.

They began to move around, collecting their bits together prior to going home. 'Maggie Telford, sir. I'm absolutely certain she's lying.' Brenda had picked up her handbag. She longed to go home but she knew she had to tell the Chief.

'Bring her in in the morning, then. I doubt if she'll run away.'

Brenda nodded. All she wanted was a shower, a drink, a snack and then bed, in that order. Andrew, she knew, would understand.

Ian pulled on his jacket, straightened the tie he had loosened and headed out of the building. He whistled tunelessly as, hands in his pockets, he made his way towards the High Street before turning into the narrow lane which led to the Green, now a conservation area from where the town had derived its name. Here, three-hundred-year-old cottages huddled around a large patch of grass with a huge oak tree in the middle. The Crown was hardly much bigger than one of the larger cottages and it had stood there for just as long. It was Ian's favourite pub. He got on well with the landlord and his wife but, more to the point, it sold a perfect pint of the local Adnam's beer. And, hopefully, his longtime friend Jim Harris would have seen to it that the first of those pints was already poured and waiting on the counter for him. With that thought in mind the decorating was completely forgotten.

Chapter Six

'Ian, it's twenty past ten. I was beginning to get worried.'
Too late Moira saw the tired lines and the greyness of
fatigue in his face. All part of the job, all understandable.
On the other hand the beery breath and the ruffled hair
were not. She could never understand why Ian's thick
hair seemed to have a life of its own when he'd been
drinking.

'I did ring to say I'd be late.' He was starving. He had
forgone the plastic-wrapped sandwich in the end. If he
wanted food, something other than he could manage to
put together himself, he would, as Short would have put it,
have to play his cards right. And it had been a very long
day, he reckoned he deserved to be spoiled a little. And he
knew by the sibilant 's' when he spoke that he was a little
worse for wear.

'Yes, but you said nine thirty.'

'I know. I'm sorry, love. But I had to speak to Doc
Harris.'

Moira, clad in the jeans and sweatshirt she had changed
into after work, sniffed knowingly. She liked Jim Harris a
lot but she also believed his second wife, Shirley, so like his
dead first one, was a saint to put up with the man. If Jim
Harris rang from the Elms after a heavy session, Shirley
Harris would drive out there and collect him without
complaint.

'It was work.'

Moira relented. If the Doc was involved there might well
be a serious injury or a death. 'Hungry?'

Ian grinned and with the added strength of the slightly inebriated slapped her on the behind a little harder than he had intended. Moira flinched. 'Yes. I'll eat whatever's going.' Just don't let it be salad, he prayed.

It was sausage casserole. Three sorts of sausage, tomatoes, chick peas and plenty of garlic. One of his favourite meals. And it was home-made, a journey into the past when Moira was content to be a housewife and mother and cooked what Ian thought of as proper, solid food: pies and puddings and cakes and biscuits. Yes, he was a slimmer and healthier man now but he did miss those meals.

'And how was the good doctor?' Moira asked as she lit the gas under the large saucepan to reheat Ian's share of the casserole.

'The same as ever. You know Jim.' Ian sat at the kitchen table where they usually ate unless they had guests. He fiddled with the pepper mill as he debated whether or not to open a can of Adnam's then decided he would. He got up to fetch it as Moira poured boiling water over the green beans. 'Those women I was telling you about, the ones receiving unwelcome telephone calls – one of them's got herself murdered.'

'Oh, Ian, how awful.' She turned to face him. 'Are they all in danger now?'

'We don't know, but we have to assume so.'

'Could it be that man you arrested?'

Ian shrugged. 'Again, we don't know. We had him in a second time this afternoon. He's got no alibi but he's acting as though he doesn't believe he needs one.'

'And where does Jim Harris come in?' She turned to lower the heat under the beans as they came to the boil.

'We're trying to find a link between the women. One of them, Pamela Richards, is his patient. Unfortunately the rest aren't on the Doc's list.' Ian knew that nothing he told his wife would go any further. As often as her best friend Deirdre tried to pump her, Moira never gave anything away.

'I still don't understand. Even if Jim Harris treated them all you couldn't possibly think he was a murderer.'

'Of course not. But one of his male patients might have met them at the surgery. He has to have met them somewhere.'

'How do you know that?'

'Because they all look alike, live alone and are around the same age. It can't be coincidence, not with six of them involved, there has to be a common denominator. And how did he get their telephone numbers? One of them's ex-directory.'

'I see what you mean. But if they had all been patients at the practice it would have been more likely that someone with access to their records, rather than another patient or doctor, was responsible.'

Ian smiled. Moira was doing what he often did himself, marshalling her thoughts verbally. 'Yes, that's it exactly. Mind you, Smithson says he took Maggie Telford out, that she gave him her number. She's the one who's unlisted, by the way, so it isn't beyond the bounds of possibility that she's lying.

'And then there's Hurst, he –'

'Hurst?' Moira interrupted as she dished up his meal. She had had no knowledge of the murder or the people involved until Ian arrived home. She had not bothered to listen to the local news that evening.

'He owns that new place, La Pêche. It's due to open on Friday. The murdered woman was working for him, she designed the kitchen. That's where the body was found, where, in fact, she was killed. Well, we already know that Hurst is connected to at least two of the women.'

'Was the Doc any help?' Moira put the plate in front of Ian. He sniffed appreciatively and picked up his knife and fork. 'Not really,' he said through a mouthful of food. 'He knows the woman, Pamela Richards, quite well, he's been her GP since she was a child. There's nothing unusual in her medical background and he says she's bright and friendly. Although the other five names meant nothing to

72

him he's promised to check in the morning to see if they're on any of his partners' lists.' It was doubtful. Only two other women had thought to include the name of their GP, and neither of them was with Jim Harris's practice. 'Tell me, Moira, where do females go in their spare time? This is absolutely delicious, by the way.'

'Thank you.' She took the chair opposite him and sat with her elbow on the table, her chin in one hand. 'You mean places where they're likely to meet on a regular basis or where someone is likely to see them regularly?' Ian nodded. 'Hairdressers, sports clubs, gyms, beauty salons, night school, women's groups. And they'd all have a record of addresses and telephone numbers. Then there are groups who meet for the cinema or theatre or shopping.'

Shopping, sports clubs, hairdressers. Pamela Richards dressed shop windows and she and Cassandra used, or had used, the same gym, the one attached to the squash club where Anthony Smithson played every week. And Janice King was a hairdresser. And Jim Hurst knew Julie Watson and Maggie Telford. These were the facts revolving in Ian's head although they still made no sense. But Moira had to be right, it had to be something along the lines she had suggested. There must be somewhere where they all went or had been, but maybe they had thought it too trivial or their visits too infrequent to include on their lists.

Enough was enough. Moira looked tired and he needed a good sleep before he faced another day of work. He stacked his plate and cutlery in the dishwasher and switched on the kettle. 'Fancy a cup of tea before we go up?'

'Yes, but I'll take mine up with me. It was busy at the garage today. Spring fever, I suspect. We sold three soft-top sports cars.' She enjoyed working in the office of the car sales showroom. None of the vehicles was second hand and all were expensive models. There was still enough money around for the garage to make a good profit and to pay her a generous salary.

Carefully carrying her cup upstairs Moira realized there would be little chance of the lounge being completed within the next week or so, not now that Ian was involved in a murder inquiry.

Ian followed a few minutes later. Tomorrow he was due to see Superintendent Thorne again. Both men were equally worried about allowing Smithson back on the streets. But there was no evidence to hold him. On the other hand there was always the reminder of the cock-up over the Yorkshire Ripper, as he'd been dubbed. Ian prayed nothing similar would happen within his Division.

It was DS Grant who informed Ian, immediately upon his arrival, that a lock-up warehouse on the Poplars Business Park had been broken into either last night or during the early hours of the morning.

'Much taken?'

'About five grand's worth of frozen meat. It's a cold storage place.'

'Just meat?'

'Yes.'

'Then put the word out to butchers and restaurants. Whoever did it might just be stupid enough to offer it to someone local.' A second later he added, 'And get someone down to the Bradley estate, someone might have heard something. They'd have needed a lorry or at least a van.' The Bradley estate was to the side of the Poplars Business Park. Recalling where his sergeant lived Ian grinned. 'You're not a witness, by any chance?'

Greg grinned back. 'No, sir. I went to bed at ten and slept like a log.'

'Okay. Get the uniforms to start digging around.'

Scruffy Short and Brenda Gibbons set off early to speak to Isobel French, née Evans. They had discovered she lived in

Ipswich. Her house was on a new estate where the gardens were still raw. Turf had been laid in some of them but it would be a while before they became established. The builders were completing the last stage of the development, a cul-de-sac of bungalows at the top of the road they were in.

Isobel French opened the door carrying a red-faced baby on one hip. She was dressed in jeans and a T-shirt and looked tired. Both Short and Brenda noticed the colour of her hair. 'Come in,' she said. 'Sarah's teething.' She kissed the baby's head. 'Every time I put her down she cries.'

Brenda glanced at John Short. Isobel's hair was very dark but she wore it short. Maybe, like many women, she had cut it after the birth of the baby in order to make life easier in at least one respect. Isobel showed no curiosity as to why they were there, she was more concerned with the baby's teething problems.

The living-room was a nondescript oblong like the houses themselves. Little thought seemed to have been put into their design. The place was clean and neat apart from a scattering of toys. The furniture had come from a discount store.

'Have a seat.' Isobel took an armchair, the baby on her knee, Brenda and Short sat side by side on the settee.

'We understand you were once engaged to Anthony Smithson. We'd like to ask you a few questions about him.' It was Short who spoke.

'Tony. Yes, I was. Why? Has he done something?'

'We don't know,' he answered honestly, 'but anything you can tell us might be useful. For instance, why did you end the engagement?'

'I was young. I thought at the time I was in love with him. I hardly knew Tony when he asked me to marry him. He sort of talked me into the engagement. Fortunately we hadn't planned to marry immediately. As the months went by I realized I had made a mistake, that I wasn't ready to make such a commitment.'

'Was there any particular incident which led you to change your mind?'

'No. I explained how I felt. Tony was hurt but he took it better than I thought he would.'

'Did he bother you at all, afterwards? With telephone calls or letters?'

'Yes, there were quite a few phone calls and letters but they eventually stopped. As I said, he took it fairly well. I saw him a couple of times after we split up and he was friendly enough. Mind you, that's some time ago now. The last time I'd already met Mike. I told him I was getting married and moving away.'

'How did he take that?'

'He wished me luck.' Isobel frowned. 'But from the look on his face I knew he didn't mean it. He must've been hurt because, you see, despite what I thought and what I'd told Tony, I got married very soon after we'd parted.' She smiled. 'This time I knew it was right, I've got Mike and now I've got Sarah.'

Which was why Smithson had only mentioned a husband and not a baby, he hadn't known about it, Brenda realized. 'Would you say he was obsessional in any way?' she asked.

Isobel pursed her lips and changed the baby's position on her lap. 'No, not obsessional. A bit pushy, maybe. He – well, I'm not sure how to explain it really.'

'He swept you off your feet?' Short suggested, the cliché, for once, apt.

'Yes, I suppose he did. Look, he must've done something for you to be asking me these questions although I can't imagine Tony getting himself into trouble. He was always pretty straight. You know, keen to get on at work, own his own place and to settle down and have a family.'

'As I explained, we don't know that he is in trouble.' Short paused before asking his next question. 'Mrs French, has your hair always been short?'

She put up a hand to touch it, staring at the Detective

Inspector in astonishment at the seemingly bizarre question. 'No. I had it cut when I was pregnant.'

Short smiled. 'Thank you. We'll be off now. If you do think of anything unusual you can tell us about Mr Smithson we'd be grateful if you'd let us know.' He handed her a card.

The baby had not cried once. She had been quite content to stare at Short, apparently fascinated by his straggling moustache which he had fingered now and then. Only when Isobel stood to show them out did Sarah start to grizzle. Short stroked her cheek, which was a mistake; she started to cry louder than ever.

'Not much gained there,' he said as he unlocked the car.

'No, but all she said seems to fit with our picture of the man.' She grinned. 'I wondered about the hair, too. And I wonder what she made of the question.'

They returned to the station. Short had another case to look at and Brenda was to contact the five surviving women. She had promised to keep in touch with them on a daily basis.

Maggie Telford chewed her bottom lip nervously. The police had telephoned to say they wanted to speak to her again, but this time on their own territory. She had been less than truthful and she had acted stupidly. The decision to be honest had not come easily, especially when she realized she might actually have committed a crime. It was all because of Brian Schofield, of course. She had never felt so much for a man, never felt that this was the one for her, and she had wanted no complications to mar the relationship. You've been an utter fool, she told herself as she waited for DCI Roper. A Chief Inspector, no less. This was serious. She was not aware that Ian had no reason to interview suspects or witnesses himself, anyone else would have been equally competent.

The door opened and a very tall man just past middle

age entered. He was handsome in a craggy sort of way. Maggie hoped he was also kind.

'Thank you for coming in, Miss Telford. I think you know why we need to speak to you again.'

She nodded. Her throat was dry. He knows, she thought, and he knows that I know too.

'This is an informal interview, but we'd like to clear up an outstanding matter.'

'Chief Inspector, I do know why I'm here.' Maggie glanced towards the WPC who was there merely to act as a chaperone. It would not do for a male policeman to interview a female alone; untruthful allegations had been made in the past, and, unfortunately, occasionally ones that were true. 'I haven't been totally honest, I'm afraid. I do know Anthony Smithson, although not intimately. We met by chance some time ago. I went out with him twice, only twice. I liked him but I didn't fancy him. I was under the impression we could be friends. However, he wasn't happy with that. He wanted far more than I was able to offer. He kept ringing me at home asking to see me again. In fact, he became a real nuisance. I thought in time the calls would stop, but they didn't.

'Then I met someone else, someone I think I can be happy with, but even though I told him this, Tony still kept phoning. I begged him not to. And then, when I read about other women receiving unwanted calls I realized it might be Tony who was making them, that it was the sort of thing he'd do. I accept his calls to me weren't obscene but some of the things he said were a bit near the mark. When he rang again on Bank Holiday Monday Brian was with me. I'd had enough, he was beginning to scare me. Brian realized what was happening and contacted you on his mobile phone whilst I kept Tony talking.'

'I see.' Ian let this new information sink in. Smithson hadn't been lying when he said he'd taken her out. It was Miss Telford who had lied. 'But why deny knowing him?'

She shook her head. 'I suppose I thought that if you

knew that I'd been seeing him you wouldn't bother doing anything about it and I'm sure you wouldn't have connected it with the other cases.'

He could see her point and it was more than likely that she really had believed he was the nuisance caller mentioned in the *Rickenham Herald*. What to do now? Charge her with obstruction? No, it would be a waste of time and the taxpayers' money. Maggie Telford had learned her lesson, he could tell that from her body language which exuded embarrassment and the high colour which had come into her face during the telling of her story. And she might be right, Smithson still might be their man in that respect even if he hadn't killed Julie Watson. Smithson's behaviour was odd. Most men, when given the brush-off, especially on such a short acquaintance, gave up much sooner than he had done. It was different with Isobel Evans, she had been his fiancée. 'Brian, I take it, is your new man. Does he know about any of this?'

'No.' Maggie touched her neatly coiled hair as if for reassurance and wondered if she ought to colour it for the time being. If Tony had a thing about dark-haired women it might put him off. 'Brian only knows what I told him, that I was receiving calls I didn't want. What'll happen to me, Chief Inspector?'

'Very little, I imagine. You have, at least, been honest now. We don't yet know whether Mr Smithson is responsible for those other calls and he did admit to knowing and making contact with you so he could be in the clear.

'I know you're aware of the murder which has been committed so I suggest you heed DC Gibbons' advice and take some sensible precautions. Stay with someone, or have someone stay with you. And please let us know immediately if you receive any more calls, even if they are from Mr Smithson.

'And, Miss Telford, a word of advice. Don't ever lie to the police again.'

The redness in her face deepened further as she stood. 'I won't. And thank you,' she said, her voice low because she was more grateful than she could express for being let off so lightly. Later that day she was meeting Brian. She would not tell him where she had been that morning but she would explain the danger she might be in and see if he could find her a room at the hotel. It was far too soon to ask him if he would stay at her house. She could commute to work from Saxborough without difficulty, and she ought to be safe enough at the surgery.

She was at the door when Ian asked, 'There's just one more thing. Where did you meet Anthony Smithson?'

'At a charity do. His firm was one of the sponsors, he was representing them and handing over a cheque. I was there as the guest of another sponsor.'

Ian made a note of the charity and the date of the event which Maggie had been able to supply as she had a pocket diary in her handbag. He felt optimistic. A charity do was a one-off affair, something all the women might have attended in one capacity or another but not thought worth mentioning. Raffle tickets, he realized, people write their phone numbers, even their addresses on the back of raffle tickets. They really might be getting somewhere.

Ian watched her go. Her back was straight but he could see it was an effort for her to keep it so. Maggie Telford was obviously in love and love did very strange things to people. And people had killed for love.

By the end of the day they were no further forward. None of the other women had been at the charity event and Maggie Telford's new version of events neither cleared Anthony Smithson nor implicated him further. Jim Hurst's background was being checked thoroughly and the contents of Julie Watson's handbag had revealed very little of the woman she had been. Ian decided to wait for the forensic team to report back from her house in Maple Grove then he would go home.

Alan Campbell had also been at the house for most of the day. After fingerprints had been taken and samples collected from clothes and surfaces, he had gone through her personal possessions and her papers, all of which were neatly filed in a cabinet in the third bedroom which had served as her office. Marriage certificate, divorce papers, house and contents insurance, car insurance and MOT certificate, were all in their relevant envelopes, clearly labelled. Julie Watson had been quite meticulous about such things. Her business papers were also in order. Paid invoices in one file, outstanding ones in another along with a copy of the one Alan had seen on Jim Hurst's desk on Wednesday morning. Yesterday morning. It seemed light years away. There were also tenders for other jobs, two of which she had been awarded but would now never complete.

'A loner I'd say, sir,' Alan said when he returned. 'Lovely house, as you'd expect. Spacious and airy with those high ceilings and everything tasteful. Well-equipped kitchen, of course. But there wasn't anything personal about the place. No letters from friends or family, no photographs or anything. It was like she existed in a vacuum.'

'That might be due to the divorce. It happens. The friends take sides or else they were mostly Matthew Watson's friends.' Alan Campbell would know all about that, Ian thought. Since his divorce some years previously there seemed to be nobody in his life. Not that he seemed too bothered about it.

'True, but there was nothing to suggest she had any sort of social life. No membership cards except one for the public library.'

Ian sighed. It made life so much harder when there was so little to go on. And what of the parents? They were flying home, landing sometime that evening, but it would be tomorrow before they reached Rickenham Green. Had there been a falling out, was that why there were no letters? Or maybe they had kept in touch by telephone. They would know when the telephone company came back to them with a print-out of calls.

Moira was surprised to hear Ian's key in the lock at six

thirty. The weather was holding and it was still warm when she had returned from work. She had spent half an hour in the garden reading the paper and sipping Earl Grey tea before listening to the news. Julie Watson had been named but there was no mention of anyone helping with inquiries. Ian did not look any happier than on the previous evening. She hoped he wasn't in too bad a mood. 'Hello,' she said, opening the fridge to pour him a beer. 'Not going well?'

'Not really, but it's early days yet.' But even as he spoke he knew that the more time that elapsed the less likely they were to find the killer. Not one person had come forward to state they had seen a vehicle in the car-park of the restaurant, but it was hardly something a driver would notice. 'Thanks.' He took the proffered glass and set it on the table. 'I'm going to change and do an hour or so on the lounge.' He slipped off his jacket and hung it over the back of a chair. 'Will dinner keep?'

'Yes. We'll eat about eight thirty if you like.' She had taken the home-made bolognaise sauce from the freezer that morning. To go with it was pasta and a green salad, neither of which would take long to prepare.

'That's fine.' Ian went upstairs to change, returned briefly to collect his beer then disappeared into the lounge, shutting the door behind him. Half an hour later Moira heard him whistling tunelessly. She smiled and picked up her book. She would sit at the kitchen table and read. The sooner he finished the papering, the better. At least the room would be ready before Mark and Yvette came to stay. Moira opened the novel and smiled. She hoped that soon she and Ian would be grandparents.

Chapter Seven

Myra Johnson sat in the small kitchen of her first-floor council flat in Magnolia House and unfolded that week's edition of the *Rickenham Herald*. On the scratched yellow formica table stood a mug of stewed tea, the way she liked it, a packet of cigarettes, matches and an ashtray.

The sun was shining but did little to enhance the inaptly named block of flats which was vandalized constantly and perennially surrounded by rubbish. Myra had lived there for so many years she no longer noticed her environment.

Lighting a cigarette she ignored the shopping in plastic bags at her feet and studied the headlines. Her heart beat faster. It couldn't be. She reread the article. A woman had been murdered and although the police were not certain it was relevant, she had been one of the recipients of those disturbing calls.

Myra scratched her head. Grey roots showed through matt black hair. I always dreaded it would come to something like this. Shocked, she couldn't believe she had thought such a thing. The woman's body had been discovered two days ago, it was amazing she had not heard the news before. But the telly had been repossessed and she wasn't a great one for the radio. They scraped by, had done so since Jack had buggered off all those years ago. Myra had recently decided that, in future, she would pay all the bills herself. Stupidly, she had been giving the last few months' rental money for the new, wide-screen set with all the extras to Luke. Only when she received the letter did she realize what had been happening. Luke, when challenged, said it wasn't a problem, that he'd sort it out and pay what was owing. He had not done so. 'Stupid sod,' she muttered as she exhaled smoke. He was the one who had sat glued to it for most of the day. Since its disappearance she had no idea what he did with himself and did not ask. She was ashamed to admit she was a little frightened of her surly son. He was out a lot more lately, which must be good for him, but where he went was a mystery. He's thirty, she thought, he ought to have a life of his own, a job, at least. It was a shame he took after his father in that respect. Myra's wages from the old people's home where she worked in the kitchen covered their expenses. It was rarely that Luke offered her any of his unemployment benefit but at least he bought his own clothes and treated her to the occasional takeaway or a packet of fags.

She heard him come in and shoved the paper into a kitchen drawer. 'You look tired,' she said, maternal instinct momentarily overriding her suspicions.

'I am. I was out late. I had some business to attend to. Is there any tea?'

Myra poured him some from the chipped pot and refilled her own mug. I can't ask him where he was, she decided, I simply cannot ask. 'Seen anything of Vicky lately?' she said instead.

'Stuck-up bitch. No.'

End of subject, Myra thought as she watched Luke, slumped in his seat, sipping his tea. 'I'm on the late shift again. I'd better get going. Would you put the shopping away for me, please?'

'Yeah. No problem.'

Waiting for the bus which would take her to work, where she would help serve up lunch – mince and mash or other food she privately referred to as slops – she tried to recall where Luke had been on Tuesday night. Not at home, that much was certain, not after seven o'clock. And how many times had she seen him in that telephone box at the back of the flats, one that was rarely vandalized because many of the occupants relied on it? Then there was the way in which he followed Vicky around, Vicky with her pert little body and long dark hair. She had to know the effect she had on men by dressing the way she did, showing off far too much of her clear, creamy flesh in those ruched, strapless tops she wore. Vicky refused to go out with Luke yet she continued to lead him on. Luke had his good points, he wasn't a drinker or gambler, and he hadn't been in trouble as far as she knew. Myra was aware that her son was good-looking, she could judge that dispassionately, as she did everything about him. But what would a future with him hold? Sweet FA, she answered herself.

What shall I do? she wondered as the bus appeared around the corner. Luke had always shown signs of obsession; once he'd fixed his sights on something he wouldn't let go until he'd got it. And there were those awful tantrums when he was younger. He'd used them as a punishment when she thwarted him. She thought he'd grown out of them, maybe he hadn't, maybe because he couldn't have Vicky he was taking it out on other women. Vicky ought to be safe, she had two older brothers who knew how to handle themselves and anyone who caused their sister problems.

I'll sleep on it, she decided as she settled back into her seat.

It was already common knowledge that the checkable fingerprints on the handle of the knife did not belong to anyone known to the police, nor did they match those of Anthony Smithson, Matthew Watson or Jim Hurst. One or other of them could have worn gloves yet the crime scene did not suggest a premeditated murder. The weapon had come from a set in the kitchen. Besides, other people would have handled the knife before it was delivered to La Pêche.

'Is he going ahead with the opening? Hurst, that is?' Short asked after the morning briefing on Friday.

'Yes. It's a strictly private do then he's got bookings from tomorrow night. The Super saw no reason to delay it,' Ian replied. And he and Moira would be in attendance. It was always possible the murderer was on the guest list. With a few free drinks inside them people were more inclined to be careless in conversation and he might learn something. Hurst was providing a hot and cold buffet which was being prepared by his new kitchen staff. Ian wondered how they felt about working in that room. 'How're the women bearing up?'

Brenda, as neat as always, was dressed in colours which complemented her chestnut hair: a tan skirt and a gold blouse. 'None of them have received any more calls and they seem safe enough at the moment. Except for Cassandra Maguire. She insists she can take care of herself.' Pamela Richards had gone to stay with her mother in Ipswich from where she could work just as easily. She had several window-dressing jobs prearranged. Janice King was with her brother and his wife, Helen Potter was at her sister's in the flat above the sandwich bar and Maggie Telford had gone to stay with her boyfriend in Saxborough.

'How come?' Eddie Roberts rubbed his scratchy chin. His razor needed a new blade and there were none in the house. He hoped his wife would remember to buy some. He was tired, too, his youngest child had had nightmares and had woken them all up twice.

'She refuses to budge from her maisonette, which is where she works. She claims no one would attempt entry from the front because all the windows are too high, which is true enough, and the door, which is at the back, and the windows there are all double-glazed with those security bolts, and she's got a chain on the door. But none of that will prevent a disaster if it turns out to be someone she knows.' Brenda paused. 'The thing is, I got the feeling that there's no one close enough to her she felt she could ask to put her up. She's very independent and has plenty of acquaintances but probably few, if any, friends.'

Ian cursed silently. It was one more thing to worry about.

'I've also checked to see if any of them use the sandwich bar but they don't.'

Detective Sergeant Grant was thoughtful. 'There's something else. Julie Watson received the last reported call not long before she died. Monday night. There haven't been any more that we know of. It could be he's picked out these six women and is following a plan.'

'Explain.' Ian couldn't see what he was getting at.

'Maybe six is the optimum number. First he scares them and then he kills them.'

'So if one of them gets another call, then she's the next victim?'

'Yes.'

'It still doesn't add up,' Brenda said, sweeping back her hair. 'People who make obscene calls usually get their kicks from the fear they induce. Their victims are unknown women, women they are afraid to face. The pattern doesn't seem right. Except the calls weren't really obscene,' she added. Upsetting, yes, frightening in that they were anonymous, but more suggestive than filthy.

'So we could still be dealing with two separate issues.' Greg voiced what they had all been thinking.

'Has Alan come up with anything, John?' Ian had put Alan to work where he was happiest, at the computer. He was going through Julie's contact lists to see what sort of premises she had worked on or tendered for work at. Maybe Alan would come across someone on that list connected to the six women.

'Not yet, he's hardly started.' Short folded his arms. 'What time are the parents due?'

'They should be here any minute. Greg, you have a word with them. They, at least, ought to be able to tell us something about Julie.'

A telephone rang. Short reached across the desk to

87

answer it. 'Okay, thanks,' he said. 'That was Andy in Forensics. None of the prints on the knife match any in the kitchen.'

Ian sighed. The knife, they knew, hadn't been wiped clean. Gloves then. But would Julie have let in a man wearing gloves? Or a woman? Yes, if she knew them.

'I can't find a thing, sir.' Alan Campbell had arrived just as Ian was wondering where they went next. 'She did a few private kitchens but most of her jobs were in commercial properties and there doesn't seem anything to link them. She's got an ad in Yellow Pages under Kitchen Design but it doesn't give her name, it's simply listed as "New Age Kitchens", nothing fancy about the name, nothing to suggest the designer is female.'

The telephone rang again. The Drews had arrived and were waiting downstairs. Sergeant Grant got to his feet, he wouldn't keep them hanging around, they must be desperate for news.

John and Margaret Drew had been shown into an empty office. They sat in tubular framed chairs with blue tweed upholstery; there was coffee in cups on the desk in front of them. If they were surprised to see the world-weary, tired-looking middle-aged man they did not show it. They were exhausted themselves from travel and grief.

Greg shook their hands and introduced himself.

'This is my wife, Peggy,' Drew said. 'Can we see her? Julie?'

'Yes. I'll arrange it for sometime later today. Are you staying in Rickenham?'

They were all now seated. 'Yes. We've got a room at the Duke of Clarence. I know we could've stayed at Julie's house, but neither of us could face it.'

Greg nodded. They were a well-preserved couple, pale beneath their tans but healthy-looking despite the emotion which showed in their faces. There was nothing brash about them, their clothes were smart but plain. 'I know how hard this must be for you both but we need to know as much as possible about your daughter in order to find the person who killed her.'

'You can't know.' Peggy's voice was shrill and edged with tears. 'We've lost both of our children now.'

Greg swallowed the lump in his own throat as memories flooded back. Had the Chief asked him to speak to them without thinking or had he been specifically chosen in the hope that it would act as a kind of catharsis? And how personal should he be? He risked it. 'I've never lost a child, but I do have some idea of what you are going through. My wife died just over a year ago.'

'I'm sorry.' John Drew bowed his head. It was difficult to accept that other people had suffered, were still suffering. 'What do you want to know? We'll tell you anything we can if it'll help.'

'What was she like? Her hobbies or interests, her friends, that sort of thing.'

Peggy Drew wiped her eyes with a crumpled tissue. 'She was a happy, contented child. You might think I'm saying that because she's . . . but it's true, or it was until Bobby died. After that she was very withdrawn, her schoolwork suffered and we couldn't get through to her. She seemed to turn against us somehow. She shut us out.'

'It wasn't her fault,' John interrupted. 'We were devastated, Bobby was only four. Instead of sharing our feelings we tried to hide them from her, to make life seem as normal as possible. We tried to protect her instead of allowing her to express her own grief.'

Peggy sighed. 'It was as if we had lost her, too. We were never really close after that. She grew up suddenly. Anyway, her schoolwork gradually began to improve and she went away to college and made a few friends. Then she met Matthew and they got married. We liked him and hoped that the marriage would solve her problems. We so looked forward to grandchildren.' She stopped. There would be no grandchildren now. With an obvious effort she spoke again. 'Julie was a solitary little girl, never a joiner. She did like the garden, though, she was always planting things and watching them grow. And she read a lot.'

Greg Grant nodded. Hence the plastic library ticket and the shelves of books Alan Campbell had described.

'We took early retirement and went to live in Portugal not long after they were married. They came to stay a couple of times but the visits were not a success.'

'In what way?' Greg ran a hand through his thinning hair. The sun was hot on the back of his neck. He moved his chair to be out of the direct rays. A picture was forming of Julie Watson: solitary, no real friends, no real interests, divorced, bitter, maybe, because of her brother's death or the break-up of her marriage. Not a happy picture, although she had seemed to enjoy her work. But whoever had killed her had gained entry into that kitchen without force. Everyone listed in her address book had been contacted, many of them already interviewed. So far they had drawn a blank.

John Drew put down the coffee he had been sipping. 'When she came to stay she was restless, unable to relax and enjoy the sun. It was as if she would rather be somewhere else, but maybe she was like that all the time. We tried to talk to her but she'd never permit the conversation to go beyond superficial matters.

'In retrospect, we wondered if her marriage might already have been rocky then.'

'Maybe Matthew couldn't get through to her either,' Peggy suggested. 'Anyway, we continued to telephone regularly. It was clear she enjoyed her work, it seemed to have given her new life. She sounded a lot more cheerful until a couple of weeks ago. Every time she answered the phone she sounded tense.'

So they didn't know about the calls. Not a close relationship then, because normally the first person to be told would be the mother. Of course, Julie may have been protecting them in the way in which they had once protected her.

'That's about it really,' Peggy continued. 'It seems so sad that there's so little to tell.'

Greg thanked them and explained that there would have to be an inquest. The Drews said they would remain in Rickenham Green until after the funeral no matter how long the formalities took. Arrangements were made for them to see their daughter later that day.

The post-mortem had taken place the previous afternoon. It revealed little they had not already known. Her death was caused by a single knife wound, one of two, hopefully the first. Had the killer been lucky or did he have a good knowledge of anatomy? The blows had been struck by a right-handed person. Grant had to remind himself that the killer might be a woman. Julie, in her nervous state, would be far more likely to admit a female. This was a possibility they had not yet discussed in full. He prayed the mortician had put her back together neatly for the parents' sake.

'That's it. We've covered everything. We've spoken to any-one with the slightest knowledge of her,' Ian said as he reknotted his tie in front of the dressing-table mirror. It was five thirty on Friday evening. He had left the station early in order to be ready for the six o'clock start at La Pêche but the traffic had been heavy and now they would be lucky to get there on time.

The bedroom curtains fluttered in a gentle breeze and birdsong could be heard in the garden. Moira closed the window prior to going out. 'I'm ready,' she said. She, too, had left work early.

'And very lovely you look,' Ian said as he kissed her.

'Thank you.' She had pinned up her hair leaving a few loose wisps to soften the effect. Her dress was lemon chiffon over satin, her sandals were gold. The only suitable thing she had to wear over the outfit was a cream linen jacket. She hoped it wouldn't turn cold again later. When the sun shone it was hard to remember it was still only May.

They drove through the town, which was busy with Friday night traffic, then took the road which led to the coast. Ian put the radio on. There was a brief mention of Julie Watson but only to the effect that the police were still appealing for witnesses to come forward which, Ian realized, was probably a waste of time in this case. But someone had to know the killer.

There were several cars in the car-park when they arrived. Ian pulled in and switched off the engine. 'It looks a bit different from the last time we were here. Come on, let's go and see what he's made of the place.' He took Moira's hand and they walked towards the open glass doors at the front.

From inside came the clink of glasses and the sound of conversation. The tables were laid and classical music played softly. Small groups of people stopped talking in order to compliment the man who was moving amongst them. Jim Hurst spotted the newcomers and came over to greet them. 'Chief Inspector Roper? I thought so. And this must be Moira. I'm very pleased to meet you both although the circumstances could've been better.'

He looks tired, Ian thought, but he did not miss the way in which Hurst's eyes took in Moira's slender figure and attractive face in one swift glance. He was proud to be with her. But was the man a womanizer? Jealousy followed pride very quickly.

A tall, statuesque woman with a dark complexion and naturally black hair approached them. 'And this is my wife, Maria.' He put his arm around her shoulders, his jacket creasing at the armpit as he had to reach up slightly to do so.

'I am very pleased to meet you both,' she said in a slightly accented, low-pitched voice. 'We understand why you need to be here but we also hope you will enjoy yourselves as well. It was so tragic. Jim has not yet got over it. We were not sure whether to continue with this tonight, that's why we took the advice of the police. We didn't want to appear callous. And we are fully booked for tomorrow night. If we turned customers away they might not return.' She held out her hands. 'We want to be a success but we hope people don't come simply because of what's happened here.'

Some would, Ian thought, the morbidly curious. They always did.

'Ah, my goodness. You have no drinks. What would you like?'

Moira asked for a dry white wine, Ian said he would have the same with some soda water. He would have to make it last as Moira hadn't offered to drive. Later he would treat himself to a proper drink. 'Shall we mingle?' Ian nodded at the increasing number of people, several of whom he recognized. He would start with those. Moira, he knew, was quite capable of striking up a conversation with total strangers, something he was never very comfortable doing.

They left shortly after eight o'clock. 'The food was excellent, wasn't it?' Moira commented.

Ian unlocked the car. 'We'll go there one evening. Let's hope the standard remains as high.' The fish dishes had been delicious.

Moira studied his profile as he began to drive. 'Did you find out anything useful?'

He shook his head. 'Not a damn thing. There were a couple of local big-wigs, a few of the Hursts' friends and people who had had some input into the business, but not one of them was prepared to talk about the murder.' He shrugged. 'It probably seemed a bit tasteless tonight of all nights.'

'Maria's originally from South America. They met in the Lake District and they've been married for almost twenty years. She's got two teenage boys and says she's very happily married.'

'Oh?' Ian grinned. Typical of Moira to have found out so much.

'Yes. She seems really nice. She also told me that Jim appreciates attractive women but she would swear he's always been faithful.' Moira laughed. 'She said that she makes sure he doesn't have the energy to be otherwise.'

If that was true it put paid to the theory of Julie Watson having snubbed Hurst's advances. 'How on earth did you find out all that in such a short time?'

'Women's talk.'

Ian wondered what Moira might have offered in exchange for that confidence then decided he would rather not know. 'I'll drop the car at home then we can walk down to the Crown. I take it you won't want anything else to eat tonight?'

'Good heavens, no.' She knew he would manage to engage in conversation with the regulars. There were two in particular with whom he would hold long discussions about football, a subject about which she understood nothing and which bored her rigid. Ian supported Norwich and had done so since he was a boy, which was anathema to anyone else who lived in Suffolk where, quite naturally, Ipswich was their team. And maybe, if he forgot about work for a while and didn't get wound up over football, she would take a leaf out of Maria Hurst's book and take him to bed early.

Maggie Telford found it strange staying in a hotel when she wasn't on holiday. Brian had been obliging enough to allow her to have a room at no cost to herself.

On Friday evening he was busy downstairs. There were the usual weekend guests plus two conferences taking place. He wanted to ensure everything was properly organized. It was his weekend on duty.

Maggie was bored. She had showered and changed, switched on the television then turned it off again. There were limits to what you could do in a hotel room. Brian had promised to meet her in the residents' bar as soon as he was free. She didn't feel like going out beforehand, although she should be safe enough in Saxborough, and she had already eaten. The food had come via room service. At least she knew what the food was like; excellent. But she could compete with that. Never before had she worried about such things. She realized she might be falling in love.

Cassandra Maguire sat at her computer tapping her short, neatly shaped fingernails against its plastic casing. The words wouldn't come and the article had to be in the post by Monday. She was covering different brands of exfoliating gel for use prior to applying a fake tan. The survey she had commissioned was beside her, along with her own findings.

She felt restless, or was it anxious? She ought to have taken DC Gibbons' advice and moved out for a while. The problem was she had nowhere to go and was ashamed to admit it. She worked on for a further twenty minutes, enjoying the early evening sunshine which streamed through the open window, then she gave up.

Her hand reached automatically for the gin and tonic beside her. She was drinking too much lately. The ice had melted but the liquid was still cold. All her acquaintances drank too much, she realized, but not enough to become totally drunk. She supposed her system was used to it because the three or four she normally had before dinner had little effect.

The telephone rang. It was a welcome distraction. If it was an invitation to go out she would accept it. There were two whole days left in which she could complete the article and she would be fresher in the morning. Besides, what was an attractive young woman doing at home, alone, on a Friday evening? 'Hello?'

'Is that Cassandra Maguire?'

'Yes, it is.' It was a male voice, one she did not recognize or did not remember hearing before.

'We're doing some research on career women. I wondered if you could spare me a few minutes.'

Cassandra groaned inwardly. Tele-sales and such people always rang at the most inconvenient time, catching you just as you got home from work or were about to sit down to eat. 'I really –'

But she was interrupted. He was giving her his name and that of the company for whom he worked. It was one of the market research firms she used herself. She knew they were reliable. 'Go on, then, if it doesn't take long.'

'I was actually hoping to make an appointment to see you. I prefer working face to face. Somewhere public of course.'

Cass hesitated for only a second. He had a nice voice, which was probably why he'd got the job in the first place. 'When for?'

'Whenever suits you.'

'Is tonight any good? I could spare half an hour, if you're in Rickenham, that is.'

'Yes, I am.'

'Shall we make it eight o'clock at the George?'

'That suits me fine.'

'Good. How will I know you?'

He gave a brief description of himself and Cass did likewise then she hung up. It was time she widened her social circle. The people she mixed with were nearly all fellow journalists or involved in the cosmetics business. Trevor Harding had probably got her name and number from some damn mailing list to which numerous people had access these days. Unless the market research people themselves had given him the name of one of their own clients.

An hour later she had eaten a makeshift meal and changed into jeans and a T-shirt. She picked up a leather jacket. The sun was setting and the evenings were still chilly.

Opening the front door she checked the balcony which ran along the length of the maisonettes and looked over the railings to see if anyone was loitering down below. Satisfied, she ran down the four short flights of steps and walked briskly out to the main road which led directly into the town centre.

The George was a red plush and panelled pub, patronized by businessmen during the week and couples at the weekend. There was no music and no gambling machines to tempt a younger clientele and signs pointed out that no drinks would be served without a glass.

Cassandra stood in the doorway where she caught the eye of a man at the bar. He smiled and made his way over to her.

The introductions over he bought her a drink and they sat at one of the tables. He made notes as they talked and he ticked some boxes on forms clipped to a pad although she couldn't see what they were. God, I sound dull, even to myself, she thought as she answered his questions.

Less than an hour later, as the place began to fill up, she was on her way home in a taxi. Alone.

It was very busy and therefore hot and stuffy in the Crown even though the casement windows were open. It was a popular pub with real ale drinkers and those who liked good home cooking, food that was actually prepared on the premises, not ready-coated in breadcrumbs and delivered from a frozen food outlet.

Ian and Moira stepped outside. 'Oh,' she said, looking up at the sky. It was dark and rain clouds had gathered. The first large drops began to fall, spotting the ground and releasing the smell of warm tarmac. 'Well, I suppose it couldn't last.'

'You'll be soaked. We'd better get a taxi.'

They hurried through the alley and up the High Street to the rank where a solitary vehicle stood waiting for a fare. Ian lengthened his stride and pulled open the back door before anyone else could beat him to it. It was almost eleven when they reached home and the rain was coming down harder. From the kitchen where Moira was making tea she could hear it drumming on the dustbin lid and gurgling down the drainpipe. At least it would replenish the water butt they used for the garden.

Her jacket was damp across the shoulders. She took it off then kicked off her sandals which were also wet and carried the two mugs through to the sitting-room where Ian was sprawled in a chair, already asleep. So much for Maria Hurst's theory, she thought with resignation.

Chapter Eight

Andrew Osborne was a solicitor, which was how he came to meet her. After the break-up of his marriage he had shown no interest in females until Brenda Gibbons came along. Their relationship had developed slowly but he still wasn't able to understand why she had chosen him and agreed to share the house they were buying together. He knew he was unattractive but he was realistic enough to acknowledge his good points. And there was nothing he wouldn't do to make that lovely woman happy.

Next weekend, he thought as he packed a holdall, next weekend I'll have her to myself. They were going to Felixstowe for three days. This weekend had worked out well although he would miss Brenda. She was on overtime because of the murder but he had to attend a course on human rights. He sighed. Another damn course. Experience counted for nothing these days, all solicitors were required to go on courses and undertake retraining in the hands of people barely out of college, some of whom wouldn't know a writ or a summons if it hit them in the face.

He rang the station to say goodbye to Brenda.

'Take care,' she said. 'I'll see you on Sunday.'

'Your beloved?' Short inquired as he rummaged in a drawer.

'Yes.' She almost added that Andrew would be away for the next two nights but Short was likely to take that as an invitation.

'He's going away?'

She swore silently. Trust him to guess. 'Some boring course.' She glanced at the clock. It was later than she had imagined. The Chief had left early to go to La Pêche but the rest of the team was still there. Alan Campbell, with nothing better to do, was continuing to sift through all the information they had obtained relating to the six women. He was certain they must have missed something, some thread which connected them. Alan glanced up as Eddie Roberts walked past his desk, pulling on his jacket. 'I'm off, we've got the wife's sister and her husband for dinner tonight. And I might even get to see my children. See you.' The door swung closed behind him.

'Well, my lovely, shall we call it a day?' Having forgotten what he was looking for, Short closed his drawer.

Brenda nodded. It would be the first time she had spent a night alone in the house since she had moved in with Andrew.

DS Greg Grant was tidying his desk unaware that everyone was leaving. 'Do you think we'll solve this one?' he asked.

John Short shrugged. 'Who knows? Day three and we're stuck already. Still, give someone enough rope and they'll hang themselves, that's what I say. Anyone hungry?'

'Why?' Brenda reached behind her and took her linen jacket from the back of her chair.

'I thought that as we're on our ownsomes tonight we could have a curry or a pizza.' He looked around expectantly.

'Yes. Why not?' Greg seemed genuinely pleased.

Brenda hesitated. Could she bear to watch the man eat and be able to eat herself? She could try. But a curry would be a mistake with the white shirt he was wearing. 'Okay, but I don't want to be late.'

The disparate trio left the building and headed towards the Feathers at the top of the High Street.

'What's it to be?' For all his faults Short was not ungenerous.

'Campari and soda, please.'

'I'll have the bitter if it's any good.'

Short ordered their drinks and they stood at the bar sipping silently for a few minutes as they began to relax. 'Why her, why Julie Watson?' Brenda said, voicing their common thoughts aloud.

'Why anyone?' There was a note of sadness in Greg's voice which suggested something more personal than the case.

'You got problems, son?'

Brenda bit her lip. How tactless. And son. Honestly. John Short and Greg Grant were about the same age.

'Only with adjusting. The last couple of years haven't been easy.'

Short swallowed some more of his drink and wiped his chin before replacing his glass in a puddle of beer on the counter. The Three Feathers had once been a smart place but over the years the Victorian-style decor had been neglected. The brass no longer gleamed, the glass lamp-shades had a thick veneer of dust and nicotine and the carpet was threadbare and sticky. But it was where they tended to congregate after work. Old habits die hard, Short had commented typically. The unkempt environment was probably natural to him. 'Problems at work, is that why you transferred?'

Leave the man alone, Brenda thought, but she did not interfere. It was up to Greg whether or not he replied. He didn't need a woman speaking up for him.

'No. My wife died.'

'Oh, shit.' Guinness spluttered from Short's mouth and wetted the front of his shirt, adding to the other stains.

Brenda closed her eyes. Shit. Hardly an expression of condolence but at least Short had avoided a plethora of clichés. And he did look embarrassed.

Greg smiled wryly. 'After that things didn't improve. My daughter'd stayed with me to help look after her but she recently left to get married and then, as soon as I got the post here, I was rushed into hospital with acute appen-

101

dicitis. On top of that I was in the middle of moving house.'

'It never rains but it pours. I think I'd better buy you another pint, mate. Why don't we all get drunk? I'd enjoy watching our lovely Brenda lose control.'

'Dream on, Inspector, I've got to drive home.'

'You could always stay with me. Ah, well, maybe not.' The look she gave him was answer enough.

'Besides, your girlfriend wouldn't approve.'

Short's eyebrows arched. He was surprised. He thought that Nancy of the plump dimpled flesh was a secret. Not that it mattered, they were both single and took their pleasures where they could find them. Neither of them was capable of remaining faithful but they shared a lot of laughter and meals and sex. Nancy had once confessed she had slept with a stranger on her honeymoon in Spain while her husband had slept off a hangover. The marriage had lasted less than a year.

'If we're not going to eat I'm going home. I'm starving.'

'The lady has a point. How about you, Greg? Is it food or more beer?'

'More beer.' Greg smiled, he looked years younger. 'But it's my shout.'

Brenda finished her drink and said goodnight. She had a very good idea how the evening would end.

Cassandra Maguire was smiling as she let herself into her maisonette. The security lights were on outside and she'd passed a neighbour on the communal stairs. There was nothing unusual to worry her. Trevor Harding was interested, she had sensed that, but he hadn't pushed his luck. Perhaps he thought she might complain if he asked her out during the course of an interview. She had been flattered but his interest had not been returned. She thought there was something vaguely familiar about him but could not place what it was. 'If there's anything else you need to know you can ring,' she had said in a businesslike voice as she stood up to leave.

It was late when she went to bed but the telephone remained silent. Neither the unknown caller nor Trevor Harding rang. She was grateful on both counts.

'I'll be back by lunchtime,' Ian said as he kissed Moira goodbye. She was still in her dressing-gown, sipping coffee at the kitchen table.

'So will I. I've got a lot of shopping to do today.'

'Do you want the car?'

'No, you take it, I'll be fine.' They had never bought a second one because parking in Belmont Terrace was always a problem and, like everyone else in the road, they had no garage. There was a bus which stopped around the corner and went directly to the town centre.

Traffic was building up as Ian set off. Rain always increased the volume and since the supermarkets had started opening their doors at eight in the morning people tended to shop earlier. The wipers hardly cleared the windscreen as the sky darkened further. Water was gathering in the road in pools by the time he reached the station and parked. Collar upturned, he ran for the entrance and pushed through the revolving glass doors, his raincoat soaked across the shoulders.

Brenda was in the general office drinking coffee and looking at the files. Nobody else was present.

Within minutes Alan Campbell arrived, eating a doughnut, a second in the grease-stained bag in his other hand.

'Anything new?' Ian asked as Brenda studied a copy of the previous night's report.

'Not concerning us.'

'Then we'll carry on from where we were yesterday.'

Despite the fact that Alan had not discovered anything relevant amongst Julie Watson's business contacts, they were going to speak to them all anyway. They had to do

103

something and they had to be seen to be doing something, however ineffectual it might be.

Problem solved? Ian wondered half an hour later upon being told that a woman named Myra Johnson was waiting downstairs to speak to him. She had come in response to the article in the *Rickenham Herald* regarding the murder of Julie Watson.

'Want me to speak to her, sir?'

Ian frowned as he thought about it. Woman to woman? Sometimes it was better, sometimes it wasn't, and Brenda was good. But Ian didn't feel properly involved yet. He decided he would speak to Mrs Johnson himself.

His initial response was that the woman who sat clutching her handbag nervously could in no way be connected with the professional women with whom they were dealing. His second thought, following almost immediately upon the first, was that this view was not only snobbish and probably insulting but also illogical.

'I had to come,' she said, her accent showing that she had never moved away from her local origin. 'There may be nothing in it, but I just had to come.'

She looked guilty; not of a crime but for being there at all. Ian smiled. 'Of course. Come with me, we'll find somewhere more comfortable.' Walking beside her, he took in the artificial blackness of the ends of her hair, the turquoise and white checked overall and the miasma of nicotine which enveloped her, yet her movements were those of a woman younger than she appeared to be. Ian guessed her life had not been an easy one.

'Would you like some coffee?' he asked once they were seated in an empty office.

'No thanks. I've got to be at work in an hour.'

'And where would that be?' Ian tried to get her to relax. He could see she was already regretting having come. Her eyes flicked around the room as if she was looking for an escape route and her tongue darted across dry lips into whose cracks lipstick had seeped.

'Sommerville, just off the Saxborough Road, the old people's home. Residential care home, I mean.'

What a sad world, Ian thought, where everyone has to think before they speak for fear of offending someone's sensibilities. Neologisms and half-baked phrases had replaced words which everyone had understood. Whatever label you attached to a thing or a person would eventually come to be regarded as a stigma anyway. And these latest phrases were most often coined by those who knew nothing of their subject, who had never lived in inner cities or amongst ethnic minorities or cared for someone ill or disabled on a full-time basis. Myra Johnson looked as though she might have done all those things.

'I'm on lates this week. I serve lunch and prepare the supper. The early shift cook breakfasts and get the lunch ready.'

'I see.' He waited.

'May I smoke?'

'Of course.' But there was no ashtray in the smoke-free zone. 'Excuse me.' Ian went out into the corridor and found a plastic container with dregs of coffee in it. It would have to suffice. He fancied a cigarette himself but he would have to wait until he was back in his own office where he tended to break the rule with alacrity. No way would he sit in one of the two small, dismal, smelly allocated rooms.

'It's my son, you see,' Myra said as she blew smoke to one side. 'Luke. He's always been a problem. Course, he's never known a father and I've always had to work hard so that might be part of the trouble.'

How many parents had he heard make excuses on behalf of their offspring? 'Tell me about Luke?' he prompted.

'Just lately he's been awful secretive.' She paused. 'And I've seen him in the phone box lots of times the past couple of weeks,' she added, gabbling the words to hide her disloyalty.

'You think he may have been making calls to these women?'

She nodded. 'And there's something else, he was out until very late on Tuesday. He said he had some business to attend to but for the life of me I can't think what that would be. And there's this girl, Vicky, he's got a real thing for her but she's not interested.'

Ian listened for a few more minutes. Myra Johnson wasn't holding back as far as her son was concerned. It all fitted: absent father, hard-working mother, thirty-year-old jobless son still living at home, a son who showed obsessional traits and had a thing for a dark-haired girl called Vicky who didn't want to know. A psychological profiler would have had a field day. Very neat. Too neat. But not impossible. Although there was the question of how Luke Johnson had met the women and got hold of their telephone numbers. But they would have to have a chat with him. 'Thank you for coming in, Mrs Johnson, we appreciate it. Can I get someone to run you to work?'

'Oh, no. There's a bus.' She looked horrified at the idea of turning up in a police car. 'You won't . . .?'

'No, don't worry. Luke won't know you've been to see us.' No mother would want her son to know she had shopped him.

An hour later Luke Johnson was slouching in a chair in interview room 4.

Maggie Telford left the surgery at eleven thirty on Saturday morning. She and Phillip Jackson had dealt with a couple of emergencies and cleaned up afterwards. 'I can't do anything until Thursday,' Maggie had told the young woman with the swollen face who was obviously in pain. The molar would have to be removed, it was the third time in as many months that an abscess had formed beneath it. 'Have a good weekend,' she had added rather pointlessly as she handed the girl a prescription for Erythromycin because she was allergic to any penicillin-based antibiotics.

Maggie needed some more clothes if she was to stay at the hotel indefinitely although she was becoming bored there. As she was already in Rickenham Green it seemed sensible to collect them on her way back to Saxborough. She felt no fear upon returning to the large, empty house. She knew who had made those calls, it was Anthony Smithson. And the police must be watching him although she could have told them he was no murderer. She was convinced that whoever had killed Julie Watson had no interest in her. She had taken the advice of the police because it seemed the easiest thing to do and it got her closer to Brian.

Through the snakes of rain running down the patio doors Maggie could see that the small garden at the back of the house was sodden. Above, the sky was pewter grey. It was just the sort of day when she wouldn't mind going back to her hotel room, making some tea and reading or watching a bit of television.

She went up to her bedroom and packed a small bag. The house was quiet and still. She felt no threat from the empty rooms nor did she jump when the stairs creaked beneath her feet. She activated the answering-machine; no messages. She picked up and scanned the envelopes which lay on the hall carpet, all were uninteresting, then she checked her appearance in the gilt-framed hall mirror: make-up perfect, lightweight scarlet suit uncreased, long dark hair still held back neatly in a pink scarf which ought to have clashed with her suit but didn't. She pulled on her olive green raincoat. It was still speckled with darker patches of moisture from her short walk from the car to the house.

Before she left she went back to the lounge and picked up a couple of new novels she had bought. Nothing had altered in her absence, not a single item was out of place, not a single fingerprint showed in the thin film of dust which had accumulated already on her highly polished furniture. The house was unviolated, just as she would be. The police would catch whoever killed Julie and that would be the end of it.

'Who haven't we seen yet?' It was getting on for lunchtime and Ian wanted to go home.

'Mark Hopkins,' Brenda replied. 'And Brian Schofield.'

A long silence followed as realization sank in.

Bugger, Ian thought. Maggie Telford's ex and her present boyfriend. These men had been, or were, very close to her. This was a glaring oversight, especially in view of her short-lived relationship with Anthony Smithson. 'I want them both seen today. John, you ring the Grand and see if Schofield's on duty. Don't let on to reception who you are because that's where Maggie's staying. I want him taken by surprise. If he's in, go and see him.' He turned to Brenda. 'Do we have an address for Hopkins?'

'Yes. He's still local. He also runs a private dental practice.'

Worse and worse, Ian thought. The women might be his patients. As much as he needed a lead he had to hope they were not. How would he explain that oversight to Superintendent Thorne? 'Alan, you pay Hopkins a visit. That's it. I'm off.' He was cursing under his breath all the way back to the car and the rain didn't help to improve his mood. It was hitting the pavements so hard that it was splashing back up again and wetting the back of his trousers.

By the time Ian had started the car Scruffy Short was on his way down the stairs. Schofield was indeed on duty and expected to be around all day. Short wasn't going to chance the receptionist's word for that, he was going now. 'Shit, bum and buggeration,' he said as the rain penetrated his jacket. He had left his raincoat upstairs but it was too much of an effort to go back for it.

At the front desk of the Grand he asked if he could

speak to the general manager. He did not say who he was in case Schofield decided he was unavailable. Surprisingly the man appeared within minutes. He merely glanced at Short's identity then led him down a long corridor to his office. 'I take it it's about Maggie,' he said.

'Yes, in a way. You were there the night she received one of those calls. Did she discuss the matter with you?'

'No. And I didn't press her to, she was upset enough as it was. And now, with the murder, well, I try not to remind her of it.'

'How long have you known Miss Telford?'

'About a month, maybe five weeks.'

'You don't mind her staying here?'

'Not in the least. Can I offer you anything to drink?'

Yes, I could murder a Guinness, he thought. But Schofield meant tea or coffee. He refused with a polite smile. Resorting to police jargon, which he never had the least compunction in using, he said, 'In order to eliminate as many people as possible from our inquiries I need to ask you where you were on Tuesday night.'

'I was with Maggie. Didn't she tell you?' He paused. 'You really can't think I'm a suspect, Inspector.'

Short grinned. 'To me, everyone's a suspect until it's proved otherwise. It's my nasty, suspicious mind, you see. It comes with the job. Just tell me where you were for the whole of Tuesday evening, please.'

'Maggie had invited me to dinner. It was supposed to be my evening off but I was late getting there.'

'How late?'

'No more than about half an hour.'

'Which made it, what time when you arrived at her house?'

'Around eight forty, I think.'

'Before that?' He had had time to kill Julie first.

'I was here, sorting out staff problems. Look, you can check if you like.'

He seems very keen for me to do so, Short thought. So I will. 'You had dinner and then what?'

'Damn. If you must know I stayed the night. It was the first time. Look, I don't like discussing Maggie like this.'

'It's better you do than have us believe you were somewhere else.'

Half an hour later Short left. He had spoken to one of the waitresses who had been involved in the dispute but she couldn't give an accurate time of its resolution. The other one was off duty. It still wasn't, and never would be, entirely certain what time Julie Watson had been murdered although it was sometime between 6 p.m. and an hour or so either side of midnight. Schofield was clear for the later times.

He's rattled, Short thought as he made his way back to the station, but maybe because, as he said, he's a busy man.

The house was set back from the road and shielded by pink-flowered shrubbery with shiny green leaves which had not yet received its first trim of the year. Alan pulled into the drive. There was obviously money in dentistry. He had rung to make sure that Hopkins was in.

Shaking the rain from his hair he rang the brass bell. Mark Hopkins' second wife opened the door with a smile of welcome. 'My husband's in here,' she said, opening the door on the right of the octagonal, wood-floored hallway. Ahead was an impressive mahogany staircase. He followed her in. It might have been raining and gloomy outside but Alan felt he had entered a warm, soft, womb-like interior. Colours ranging from pale honey to amber toned and blended, and soft, concealed lighting gave the impression of summer.

'Mark, DC Campbell is here.'

'What? I'm so sorry.' He stood, laying down *The Times* and removing his glasses as he did so. On the table beside him was a glass of whisky.

'Do you want me to stay?' Lorna Hopkins asked as she

hovered in the doorway. She had no idea why the police wanted to see her husband.

'It's up to you, sir.' Alan turned to the dentist, who shrugged. He was a short, plump man with hair already turning white and a neatly trimmed beard flecked with ginger.

'Perhaps you wouldn't mind making us some coffee, Lorna,' Hopkins suggested gently.

Something to hide? Alan wondered. 'I need to ask you a few questions concerning your first wife, Maggie.'

'Certainly. Do sit down.' He frowned as he lowered himself back into his armchair. 'Nothing's happened to her, has it?'

'No.' Alan explained about the telephone calls.

Hopkins stared at him. 'You're suggesting I made them?'

'I'm not suggesting anything, sir. Can I ask you about your relationship with her?'

'We met not long after we'd both qualified. We were at one of those boring dental conventions. She was great fun. We skipped most of the meetings and did our own thing. We were young, Constable, ambitious, too. We married, only to discover that we should have remained as friends who enjoyed a good time together.

'You might find this hard to believe but we parted amicably. We both had money; we were lucky enough to have come from privileged families and we were both in private practice. We settled our finances and went our own ways. A year later I met Lorna.'

Lorna, wife number two, did not resemble Maggie Telford in any way. She, like her husband, was short, but blonde and well rounded and would become fatter with age. Mark Hopkins could not have been accused of having a preference for brunettes.

'Are you still in touch with your ex-wife?'

'No. I have her address and telephone number, as she has mine, but we got out of the habit of ringing each other long ago. And, strange as it seems, we haven't even run

111

into each other by chance. I'm more of a home body now.'

He stood just as his wife reappeared carrying a tray; she placed it on the walnut sideboard then began to pour.

'This is why,' Hopkins continued as he reached for a framed photograph of two small, very blonde girls. 'Jasmine and Hatty. Harriet, actually.'

There was no sign of twin infants; no noise, no mess, no toys. Maybe there was a nursery with a full-time nanny.

'Lorna's mother's just collected them. She'd have them all the time if Lorna would let her. My wife doesn't work, she wants to stay at home at least until they're both settled in school. Ah, thank you.' He reached for the cup he was handed.

Alan did the same. He had been wrong about the set-up and was proved more so when Lorna said, 'After you rang I rushed around throwing all their bits in a basket. The place isn't always this pristine.'

'How else can I help you?' Hopkins said, knowing there had to be more to the visit than questions about his previous marriage.

'Can you tell me what you were doing on Tuesday night?'

'Tuesday? Haven't a clue. Can you remember, darling?'

Alan turned to Lorna. Her eyes were half-closed in concentration. 'Yes. You brought Peter back for a drink. I was bathing the children so it must've been about quarter to six.'

'Peter's my partner. He's a lot older than me. Never married, but every so often he seems to enjoy a dose of domesticity and Lorna's excellent cooking.'

'Like your other stray dogs,' she said with an understanding smile.

There was harmony there, Alan saw. He had heard that second marriages often worked out better than the first but he was not going to find out for himself. He fingered his top lip, still unused to the smoothness now that he had shaved off his moustache. It had been grown to add some

112

gravitas to his appearance but it was so fine it had made him look younger. 'Peter who?'

'Jones. What's this about, Constable?'

'Do these names mean anything to you?' He listed five, not including Maggie's.

'Not a thing. Why?'

'They're not, nor ever have been, patients of yours?'

'No.'

'How about your partner's?'

'You'd have to check with him but I don't recall seeing any of them on the computer.'

Alan made a note to do so. 'What time did Mr Jones leave on Tuesday?'

'He didn't.'

'It was one of those nights,' Lorna interrupted. 'We had another couple over for dinner as well and Peter wasn't in a fit state to drive. He stayed the night and he and Mark went in to work together in the morning.'

To be on the safe side he took the couple's name and address and said he would leave them in peace. Hopkins showed him to the door. 'I don't like to appear thick, but why those questions?'

'We're interviewing everybody we think might be able to help us with a case we're working on.'

'Good God.' Hopkins gripped the door jamb with white knuckles. 'That poor woman who was murdered?' His face was pale. 'But why me? I don't even have the faintest idea who she was. Hold on, was she getting phone calls too?'

'Yes.'

'And you think Maggie is in danger, that's it, isn't it? You think I'd wish her harm?'

'We have to check every possibility, sir. Thank you for your time. I'm sure Mr Jones will confirm what you've told me so it's doubtful we'll need to trouble you again.' As he turned to walk back to the car he could hear Hopkins say, 'Lorna, you won't believe . . .' before the door was closed behind him.

Chapter Nine

Once again Brenda Gibbons and John Short were the last to leave the station on Saturday evening. Both of them were tired, more from frustration than lack of sleep, and Short was making heavy work of recovering from his hangover. He had tried to disguise it from Brenda but the greyness hadn't left his face all day.

By lunchtime she and Greg Grant, also suitably hung over, had spent an uninspiring hour and a half with Luke Johnson. Greg had now gone home to recuperate.

'Johnson's got no form,' Brenda told Short, 'but he doesn't seem to have an alibi either. If he has he's not saying, because he refused to answer any questions even though he hadn't been cautioned. He supplied his name and address, which we knew anyway, then clamped his mouth shut.' They had let him go, knowing that he would be back.

'I had about as much luck with Schofield. Alibied after eight thirty, and possibly before if we can get hold of the other waitress.

'You can buy me a drink, Miss Gibbons, if you'd like to make an old man happy, hair of the dog and all that, then you can tell me what you really think of the chance of Luke Johnson's being guilty.'

'I'm going home, Mr Short, sir. I'm expecting a call from Andrew.' She felt herself blushing as he leered at her. This was a deviation from the hard persona she had adopted by way of protection from further knocks, the only one her colleagues had come to know.

'You've got a mobile phone, he can get you on that. Besides, you might as well enjoy yourself, who knows what your man's up to in Manchester or Birmingham or wherever he is.'

Having a drink with Scruffy Short was not her idea of enjoyment and there was no point in trying to explain that Andrew wasn't like that, Short would assume she was kidding herself. Yet for some reason she found herself walking beside him up the High Street. Perhaps it was the thought of the empty house. After years of living alone, she had not expected to miss Andrew so much.

It was still raining, but not so heavily. Traffic swished past and people hurried home in the gloom, dodging the raindrops which fell from window ledges overhanging the pavement. Short's grey raincoat, which he had remembered to put on this time, had greasy stains down the front; Brenda's tan one, which she wore belted at the back, was fresh from the dry-cleaner's.

When they reached the Feathers people were already eating. How they could do so with the smell of over-used cooking oil hanging in the air and mingling with cigarette smoke was beyond Brenda. Tonight was added the pungency of damp clothing. There were far nicer places in which to drink . . . yet they kept going back. Brenda ordered a pint of Guinness and a Campari and soda and handed over the correct money before perching herself on a bar-stool. Short preferred to stand. Maybe the drink went down more easily when he remained on his size ten feet.

'So it's just you and me,' he said with a grin. 'The stuff dreams are made of.'

'Yours, not mine.'

'No harm in hoping. Luke Johnson,' he said, changing the subject abruptly and glancing around to make sure no one was within hearing distance, 'he's pond life, all right, but is he our man?'

Pond life. She wondered why he picked up such expressions only after they'd become hackneyed. 'Is that a rhetorical question?'

'No. I would like your considered opinion.'

'I can't see it. He's hiding something though. When we mentioned La Pêche and the murder he was visibly shaken.'

Short nodded as he sucked Guinness froth from his moustache. 'But who wouldn't be if they believed themselves to be a suspect, especially if they were innocent.'

'I don't think the word innocent applies to Luke Johnson. He's guilty of something, why else keep quiet, and why not provide an alibi?'

'Be fair to the man, oh beautiful damsel, we don't know that he hasn't got one. Just because he refused to answer our questions doesn't mean he hasn't got dozens of witnesses to swear to his whereabouts. And if he was home, alone, watching the telly, he knows we're not going to believe him.'

'True, but even his mother suspects him.'

'I imagine his long-suffering mother would be only too grateful to see him locked up for a while. Ah, well, he'll talk sooner or later, they all do.'

Tomorrow, Sunday, they intended speaking to Vicky; Victoria Dennis, Mrs Johnson had told them. Brenda wondered what the Chief thought of it all. Unusually, he hadn't come up with a single theory, however improbable. There were still people they hadn't interviewed: the staff at the gym and the librarian who was usually on duty when Julie Watson returned her books. People met in public libraries, especially if they were regular users. Cass Maguire had been going there recently to use the reference section for an article she was putting together on cosmetics over the centuries. Janice King was also a member.

'The net is being cast wider. We're bound to catch something, even if it's only a cold.'

'God help me, ' Brenda muttered. How on earth did his woman put up with him or his conversation?

'What's up?'

She shook her head and sighed. If he didn't know there was no point in telling him.

Short bought the second drink then said he had to go because he was meeting someone.

'Work or pleasure?' Brenda hooked her bag over her shoulder and finished the last of her Campari and soda. Short shuddered as she ate the slice of lemon, rind and all.

'Curiosity killed the cat,' he said.

'Your redhead, I suppose.' She turned away with a smile at the look of surprise on his face. The WPC had been right, Inspector Short's sex life was no longer the secret he had believed it to be.

She put up her umbrella and made her way to the car, and, forgetting the sunshine earlier in the week, wondered how long it would be before summer arrived.

Ian, as promised, had returned by lunchtime but the house was empty. He stood in the kitchen watching the rain slanting across the garden. The bushes swayed and, in the stillness, he could hear the patter of water on their large, flat leaves. There was no excuse not to finish the decorating, it was too wet to go anywhere and the football season had just ended so he couldn't watch Norwich. There would be sport on television, there always was, but he preferred watching it live in the open air in the atmosphere of a cheering, or otherwise, crowd. The case was very much on his mind. He couldn't help feeling that they had had the killer within their grasp and let him go. But which of the men it was, he did not know. With the help of his girlfriend, Matthew Watson had finally come up with an alibi for Tuesday night. This did not seem suspicious to Ian, who could rarely remember where he had been or what he had eaten the night before.

The news of his ex-wife's death had obliterated all Watson's memories for a while. Only on the day after he had identified her had he remembered that Debbie had met him from work on Tuesday; they had done some shopping then gone home to eat, after which he had completed his arguments for the meeting which had taken place on Wednesday morning. They had gone to bed at the same time and left for work in the morning together. Debbie had confirmed this but there was always the chance her boyfriend could have left the house and returned without her knowing whilst she was asleep.

The back door swung open, bringing him back to the present. 'You're soaked. Here, let me take those.' Ian reached for the shopping bags.

A bedraggled Moira stepped into the kitchen and shook the rain from her hair. 'Would you believe it! I'd finished the shopping and just missed one bus. The next one came but the damn thing broke down. The driver radioed in for a replacement but I decided to walk. Then the bags got too heavy to carry in one hand so I couldn't use my umbrella.' She took off her three-quarter length waterproof jacket and slung it over the back of a chair from where it dripped on to the floor.

'I'll make some coffee,' Ian said to placate her. It was unusual for Moira to be in a bad mood. 'You go and change.'

A few minutes later she reappeared in jeans and a pale pink sweatshirt. She seemed a lot happier. 'Have you got any plans for the rest of the weekend?'

'The front room. I think I can get it finished today.'

'Good. Then perhaps, whatever the weather, we can go out for the day tomorrow.'

'Good idea.' So that was it. In the early days of their marriage Moira had been tied to the house and to caring for Mark, and he had put in long hours to get where he was. But that was in the past. As Chief Inspector his work should have entailed fewer hours and more desk work but he did not like to operate that way. Moira believed that the time had come when they should be seeing more of each other and she was right. Ian realized he ought to know better than to take her for granted. She was younger than him and very attractive. 'Why don't we drive down to the coast and have lunch somewhere?'

'It's a deal.'

They ate sandwiches and drank more coffee then Ian got to work. Moira did the ironing and listened to a play on Radio 4. She couldn't wait to be able to sit in the front room in comfort again.

At ten to six Ian stood at the kitchen sink rinsing wallpaper paste from his brush. He washed and dried his hands and turned to Moira with a smile. 'All done. Come and have a look.' He took her by the arm and led her up the hall.

'It's really lovely,' she said, and it was. His one previous attempt at papering had been adequate, no more than that. Fortunately only she had noticed the place where the pattern didn't quite match.

The front room ceiling had been repainted white along with the area above the picture rail. The mouldings around the fitting which held the central lights had been picked out in pale green and dusky pink which mirrored the muted colours of the paper which she had chosen. With the dust sheets removed and the furniture back in place the room looked completely different. They had become so settled in Belmont Terrace Moira doubted they would ever move now.

Ian kissed the top of her head. 'I'm glad you like it. Now why don't we pop out and celebrate before we eat.'

Over a couple of pints of Adnam's Ian brought her up to date with the Julie Watson case but for once Moira had nothing to say about it. No one had yet been able to come up with a theory. He had hoped, as had happened before, that her feminine intuition, which he never doubted, would latch on to something he was unable to see.

The rain had eased to a drizzle. By the time they returned with a Chinese takeaway it had stopped altogether. A fresh wind was blowing, scattering litter and cherry blossom and drying the pavements.

* * *

Cassandra Maguire, her long dark hair loose about her shoulders, sat in front of her computer screen on Saturday evening with a feeling of satisfaction and the knowledge that she now had Sunday in which to relax. She had been right to leave the article last night and come back to it fresh today. It was finished and would now be in the post by Monday as per her deadline.

She got up and stretched, easing the tension from her shoulders. She had no plans for the evening, much of her socializing was done during the week. I'll have a shower, get undressed, have something to eat and go over my research, she decided, itching to get on with the manuscript which she hoped would be published as a book. The text was nearing completion and she had already found an illustrator. She might ring some friends and make arrangements to meet on Sunday. She had earned some fun.

An hour later, in silk pyjamas and a matching robe, she went to the maisonette's tiny kitchen to prepare a meal. It would be, as it mostly was, a ready-made meal from the supermarket. As she had told DC Gibbons, her culinary skills were barely adequate.

Opening the fridge door she took out a waxed packet. 'Not only lazy, but boring,' she scolded herself. Glancing out of the window she noticed it was raining again.

The telephone rang just as she sat down to eat. She reached for the receiver, spoke a few words and ended the conversation quickly.

It was eight thirty when the doorbell rang. It wasn't yet dark but the low, heavy cloud had caused the light-sensored bulbs to become activated. Through the patterned glass Cass saw the outline of a man of medium height and medium build. She opened the door the four inches the chain allowed. 'Trevor, I explained I was busy . . .' She had told him so over the phone. She stopped, her explanation sounded feeble now that he could see she was in her nightclothes. She took the chain off and opened the door fully. 'Look, you can come in for a coffee, but I really am working.' She indicated the papers on her desk and those scattered to one side of the multi-coloured striped settee where she had been sitting.

'It's not coffee I want,' he said.

Minutes later she realized that a reputable market research company would not go about its business in the way in which Trevor had done on Friday evening before she recalled it was she who had suggested the meeting. And then, as he spoke, she knew why his face had seemed familiar when his name meant nothing and where it was she had seen him before.

Helen Potter was grateful to her sister, Jill, for putting her up but she would be glad to get back to her own flat. The accommodation over the sandwich bar had two bedrooms but with three adults in occupancy the small place felt cramped. Jill had changed since her marriage to Mike. Once as fun-loving as Helen, she was now content to work then spend the evenings watching television. This was the fourth such evening the three of them had passed in this manner. If only Darren, her boyfriend, wasn't away she wouldn't have had to move out of the flat they shared. Friends had invited her out that evening but Helen was more scared than she liked to admit. The idea of some stranger out there waiting for her was causing her to lose sleep.

At eleven she rang her answering-machine to pick up any messages, hoping that Darren might have called. Someone had rung, had listened to her message, waited a few seconds then put the phone down again. Nothing had been said but she was sure she had heard breathing. She shivered. Yes, she could watch endless television if it meant staying alive.

'Ring the police,' Jill advised her. 'It might be innocent but you can't take any chances.'

At eleven thirty an officer arrived to accompany her to her flat. They would try 1471 but if it was the person they were seeking it was likely that the recording would tell them that the caller had withheld their number.

'Sorry, love,' the PC said when this was the case. 'Is there anyone you can think of who'd be ringing so late?'

Helen shook her head. 'No, not without leaving a message. It was him, I know it was.'

'We'll take you back to your sister's now,' he said, wondering if the pale-faced brunette had been marked as the next victim.

Back at the station he rang the Chief at home as he had been instructed to do if there were any developments, no matter how insignificant they might seem.

Ian listened and, like Helen Potter, felt certain that whoever had rung her was the man they were after. He sighed, sure he was in for a restless night. The late call to Helen had been timed at ten fifty-six by her answering-machine. It could have been a wrong number, it could have been anyone. Either way they would keep an eye on her. Although not religious, Ian prayed there would be no more victims.

Not having received a reply to her daily telephone call on Sunday morning, Brenda had driven to Cass's place and rung the bell. There was no answer. She had peered through the kitchen window next to the front door but saw nothing other than some unwashed dishes on the work surface. No lights were on, no curtains were drawn. She questioned the neighbours. One of them had seen her car drive off about nine on Saturday evening. Brenda was furious. Cass might be independent, but how could they keep an eye on her if she didn't at least ring to say she was going away? She was still annoyed when Andrew returned early on Sunday afternoon. She started to discuss the case with him, knowing it was unfair.

'Pubs?' Andrew suggested as the common denominator when Brenda had asked his opinion. He was tired but delighted to see her again. 'Lots of people meet in pubs.'

'Mm.' She watched him take off his suit and change into jeans and a polo shirt. The weather had changed overnight. The sun was shining again and they were going to walk along the beach then have a drink in their local which remained open all day. It was the sharing Brenda enjoyed so much, the mutual taking care of things which she had never had with her alcoholic mother or her violent, bullying husband, the sharing of chores and ideas as well as meals and a bed. 'I agree it's where a lot of people meet, but you don't give your phone number to a stranger. And despite what I thought before, it has to be a stranger.'

'Why?' Andrew pulled a thin woollen sweater over his head.

'Because none of these women know each other and they move in different circles. No one name crops up on their lists of friends, family and acquaintances, nor have they shared the same repair man or builder. We've questioned everyone they know, we've interviewed the women again but they still can't provide the name of anyone else close to them.'

'I get your point. Now listen, gorgeous, I've spent the last two days discussing human rights and the law and you've been hard at work. Today is for us, what's left of it.'

'You're right.' Brenda stood up. She wasn't being fair to Andrew but she couldn't stop thinking about Julie Watson and what she hoped would not become the fate of the others. She reached up, pulled his head down and gave him a long, slow kiss.

Hand in hand they walked along the sand at Southwold. Old-fashioned beach huts were lined against the wall. They carried their shoes and let the gentle waves wash over their feet but the sea was still cold so they moved up the beach.

They didn't talk much, they had no need to fill the companionable silence with words. Andrew was wondering how long it would take him to persuade Brenda to marry him, Brenda was wondering how long it would take to solve the case, if it was solved. And something Andrew had said earlier had triggered a connection in her brain but she could not work out what it was. The best thing was to forget it and enjoy the moment. If it was important it would come back to her.

A few miles away, in Aldeburgh, Ian and Moira were sitting on a bench outside a pub watching the same stretch of sea. They, too, had walked and then eaten a late lunch. Ian's only regret was that he was driving and therefore had to curtail his input of Adnam's real ale.

Chapter Ten

By the middle of Monday there was more information to hand than they knew what to do with but none of it married up. Names and addresses and the backgrounds and histories of scores of people had been fed into the computer and cross-matched. Alan Campbell, his face creased in concentration, was hunched over his screen, heedless of the ache across his shoulders. One thing, anything, he told himself, and we can take it from there. It seemed impossible that so many facts could amount to nothing.

Eddie Roberts had spoken to Vicky Dennis on Sunday morning. She had still been in her none-too-clean dressing-gown when he arrived at ten past eleven and was totally unconcerned about her appearance or the fact that a woman, not much older than herself, had been murdered.

'Yeah, Luke's a pain,' she had admitted when asked about her relationship with him. 'It's not like he's a teenager, you'd think he'd have grown out of it by now.' She had been speaking from the untidy living-room of her one-bedroomed flat in a block diagonally opposite Magnolia House. 'Look, if he's done something then I don't know about it. I don't speak to him if I can help it.'

But you enjoy his attention, Eddie calculated correctly. Through the tightly belted robe he could see how shapely she was and even though last night's mascara was smudged beneath her eyes and her hair was still tangled from sleep she was a looker and obviously trying to flirt with him. Eddie left this last observation out of his report. His own wife, pretty, if plumper since the children, and both of their extended families were enough to cope with. He knew that he was fairly unusual in that he was a one-woman man.

The Chief had listened to Eddie with a grim expression. Someone, surely, had to slip up soon. 'Alan?' Ian repeated as he shook his head in puzzled admiration for anyone so adept in technology. DC Campbell was in a different world when in front of that screen.

'Sir?' He swung around in the swivel chair and faced the rest of the team. Half-empty coffee cups littered the desks. Short passed Alan a packet of biscuits. He took two and bit into one of them. His diet was abysmal, worse than Short's, but although he appeared anaemic and under-weight he had never had a day off sick and he sailed through his medicals. On the plus side he rarely drank and did not smoke.

'How did it go yesterday?' No progress had been made, Ian wasn't expecting good news.

'The staff at the gym weren't much help. According to their records Julie Watson has never been a member there and as the place has only been open about fifteen months it wasn't hard for them to check. However, one of the trainers there does know Cassandra Maguire. He planned her individual fitness programme and she usually works out once or twice a week. Pamela Richards is on their books, too, but her name didn't mean anything to the people I spoke to – though she admitted she only went a couple of times.'

'Is this fitness trainer a likely candidate?'

'Hard to say, sir. He's married with a baby daughter, information he volunteered readily enough, and he works full time at the gym. He didn't come across as if he had anything to hide, but that was only my impression.'

'Get someone to check him out anyway.' Anyone who admitted to knowing any of the women was a candidate.

'And the librarian?' Ian asked. Alan had made an appointment to see her at her bungalow on Sunday afternoon.

'Susan Pritchard. She's been at the library for years and remembers Julie well. She always changed her books on Fridays somewhere between four thirty and six, depending on work, I assume. If the library wasn't busy she and Julie would chat. Mrs Pritchard said she thought Julie was a lovely person but that she might have been lonely.

'Anyway, as to noticing her speaking to anyone else, she didn't think so. Julie was never there long. Apparently she had about half a dozen or so favourite authors and usually stuck to them rather than studying the racks.'

'And the other staff?'

'Mostly female but there are two males. One's a trainee, he's only been with them for a few weeks, the other one's on the point of retirement. Mrs Pritchard thought the younger of the two was "a bit wet behind the ears", her words, but would probably shape up in time. She said Geoffrey Peterson, the older man, was kind and gentle, happily and quietly married with three children and four grandchildren.'

'It's the quiet ones you have to watch,' Short offered predictably. Equally predictably his words were ignored.

Ian knew that none of these people were probable candidates but nor could they be ruled out without further inquiries. 'Did Mrs Pritchard recall ever seeing Cassandra Maguire?'

'No, not even when I explained what she does for a living. The reference library is upstairs, it's a completely separate department.'

'All right, let's concentrate on Luke Johnson for the moment. Find out where he was on Tuesday night. Ask around the estate, knock on doors, make your presence felt but don't speak to him directly. Make it clear it's a murder inquiry, that should get the tongues wagging and, hopefully, push him into making a mistake.

'Eddie, you and Grant go over there now. You can join them, Brenda, when you've made your calls. That's it.' Ian left the room and went to his own office to face another pile of paperwork.

Alan Campbell picked up the telephone. He was still checking Jim Hurst's background, looking into his previous business in the Lake District and liaising with the local police in case there were any unsolved cases of obscene telephone calls or murder which had occurred during the time he lived there. His reasons for moving might not have been the ones he had given. And he was a relative newcomer to Rickenham Green; the telephone calls had begun after his arrival. Clutching at straws, Alan thought, smiling, knowing that John Short would have said exactly the same thing.

On his way upstairs Ian thought over what Hurst's wife, Maria, had told Moira. Her confidences, considering she had only just met Moira, seemed a little suspicious. Were they meant to be passed on to Ian in the hope they would provide some sort of character reference? Or was it that, as a foreigner, she was less reticent about discussing such matters? He grinned to himself. Had he voiced that thought to Moira she would have accused him of xenophobia, a fault he tried to overcome but couldn't. It had been a shock when he learned that his son was to marry a French girl. He had met the family just before the wedding in Reims. They were sophisticated, hospitable and very wealthy and they had been delighted to meet Mark's family.

For French people they weren't bad, had been Ian's niggardly opinion.

By Monday morning Maggie Telford was glad to be back at work. Being waited on was nice but she missed being amongst her own things. She would stay one more night then return home. She told Brenda Gibbons as much when she received her daily telephone call which she took at the surgery that day.

'We can't force you to stay at the hotel, but it might be best for the moment,' Brenda told her.

'I'm not sure that it's any safer, you know. There're people coming and going all day and until late at night. Anyone could walk straight up to my room without arousing suspicion. Besides, I can't rely on Brian's generosity indefinitely.'

Brenda had wondered about that. Maggie's boyfriend, or lover, whatever she called him, was the general manager, not the owner. The hotel was part of a chain which made millions of pounds in profit over the course of a year. She supposed, as far as the bookkeeping was concerned, Brian could lose this small additional expense somewhere. Not my problem, she thought as she put down the phone.

Maggie checked her appointment book and waited for her next client. Brian was off next weekend and they planned to go away somewhere. As she hadn't seen much of him over the weekend it was something to look forward to, although she realized the irony of the situation; they would be in another hotel. He had visited her room as often as possible and met her in the bar during his breaks. Until she had witnessed it at first hand she had had no idea how much the job entailed. There were three bars, four function rooms, the restaurant and a snack bar. There was also a swimming pool and gym facilities, all of which had to run smoothly. This was apart from the cleaning of the rooms, the overseeing of the staff and dealing with the customers themselves. She had lost count of the number of times she had heard the words 'Would Mr Schofield please come to reception.' No wonder, when he had slid into bed beside her late on Saturday night, he had struggled to respond to her touch. This was another reason why she wanted to return home, an unselfish reason. Last night Brian had joined her in the residents' bar for a nightcap. In retrospect she realized he would sooner have gone straight to bed. It was unfair to expect him to entertain her when he was exhausted. Far better for him to come to her when he was rested and in the mood for her company.

'How's the bridge?' she asked with a professional smile when the client was settled in the chair. Placing a mask over her own nose and mouth Maggie began a routine dental check-up as she gently manipulated the angled mirror between teeth and gums and pondered the mysteries of life, or one of them in particular. What was it about a person that made you fall in love with them?

Myra Johnson was on her way to work when an unmarked police car pulled up outside Magnolia House. Two men got out and crossed the litter-strewn patch of grass and headed towards the double front doors with their mesh reinforced glass panels which someone had still managed to crack. A spider's web pattern decorated them both. Myra didn't even hesitate. If the police wanted to speak to her, and she knew instinctively they were police, they knew where she worked. She had told the tall one with the thick hair and the nice face. It was bound to be Luke they wanted. He had said nothing about being interviewed which was good because it meant he hadn't guessed her part in it. If only he'd get a job, she thought, although he was far from alone. Two thirds of the residents on the estate were in the same position. It was as if the hopeless spirit of the buildings themselves seeped into their bones by osmosis. If she didn't have her job Myra believed she would go mad or give up herself. She turned the corner and waited for the bus.

Eddie Roberts and Greg Grant were aware of the short woman with the dyed black hair who had glanced at them then continued walking. Over her clothes she wore a standard issue turquoise and white checked overall. 'Luke's mum,' Greg commented although he had not met her. They were not to speak to her either, it might cause problems between mother and son and the Chief seemed to think Myra Johnson had troubles enough.

Luke had not offered any sort of an alibi but from what Myra Johnson had told them he probably had no friends to provide him with one. They were certain he was guilty of something even if it wasn't either of the crimes they were working on.

'Been here before?' Eddie asked as he pushed open one of the swing doors.

'No.'

'Then you're in for a treat.'

'Yes, I see what you mean.' Greg Grant wrinkled his nose as he took in his surroundings. The predominant aroma in the concrete entrance hall was urine; beneath that were undertones of rotting rubbish which emanated from several split black bags in a corner. The bass notes were dampness and mould. Above the green verdigris on the walls was some highly unoriginal graffiti which Greg read before following Eddie towards the lifts. There were two of them and both were unusually operational. 'Immediate neighbours first,' Grant said, taking control without abusing his rank. He liked Eddie but thought he might be a little too easy-going.

They each knocked loudly on the doors adjacent to Mrs Johnson's flat. If Luke was at home he would hear them. No one responded to Eddie's knock so he tried the flat across the hall.

Greg Grant was luckier. The elderly woman who squinted at the Sergeant's identity through the crack in the open door created by the safety chain grunted. 'Is it about the vandalism?' she asked as she let him in. 'I'm Dorothy Edwards, by the way.'

'No, it's a bit more serious than that, Mrs Edwards.' She was wearing a wedding ring.

'You'd better have a seat then. Do you want some tea?'

'If it's no trouble.'

Grant sat on an old horsehair-stuffed wing chair. He had accepted the offer of tea because the woman was receptive, prepared to talk. From what he had learned of the residents of Magnolia House from Eddie in the car on the way over he had anticipated slammed doors and sullen silence.

The front door opened into the living-room; to the side was another door through which Mrs Edwards had disappeared and beyond which was a passage presumably leading to bedroom, bathroom and kitchen. The living area was neat but shabby and Mrs Edwards owned a preponderance of silk and plastic flowers that far exceeded the norm.

She returned within minutes bearing a tray containing two mugs, a bottle of milk and a packet of sugar. Dorothy had long since given up on the niceties of life. The tea was a shade of dark orange and was served with full cream milk. Greg tried not to gag. He liked weak tea, China if possible, and the fully skimmed milk to which he had become accustomed once his daughter had taken over the housekeeping responsibilities from her mother.

'If it's not the vandalism, not that I think you'll ever stop it now, what's it about?'

'What can you tell me about Luke Johnson, Mrs Edwards? I take it you know him.'

She nodded as she gripped her tea in both hands as if she was cold. 'Yes, since he was a small boy. She came here, Myra, that is, about twenty-five years ago, just after me, in fact. This place was relatively new then and we were all grateful to be housed here. Hard to believe now, isn't it? Anyway, it was the usual story, her husband had left her and she'd been living in a bedsit because she couldn't afford the rent where they were. Her name finally came to the top of the housing list and she found herself here.

'She's a worker, she keeps the pair of them going and always has done. I don't think that boy's ever had a job in his life. He's quiet, though, I'll give him that. No loud music late at night and now, of course, the TV's been repossessed. Even as a child he never made much noise, unlike some of the others.'

Greg replaced his mug on the tray which stood on the

small table between their identical wing-back chairs. Rude it might be, but it was impossible for him to drink the tea.

What Dorothy had told them was no more than they knew already. 'Does he have any friends? Anyone who calls when his mother's not in?'

'None that I've ever seen or heard. And I would hear, mark my words. These walls are like cardboard. It's not too bad today but sometimes you can hear babies crying and people's television sets. And the man downstairs drives me mad listening to Radio 5 full blast most of the day, unless he goes out.' She paused and looked towards the window.

Greg looked in the same direction. He could see rows of washing on lines at the top of tall poles and some garages which, knowing the area, may well have held items other than cars.

'What's Luke supposed to have done?'

'We don't know that he's done anything illegal, we think he might be able to help us.'

Dorothy Edwards laughed and slapped her leg. 'That old chestnut. You wouldn't be here, Sergeant, if you didn't think he'd been up to something, you'd have asked him yourself. Look, the only serious crime I've read of recently is the murder of that poor woman and I can't see him being mixed up in that.'

'There's a chance he knows something about it.'

'Well, you've obviously got your reasons for thinking so. He's never caused me any problems but I've heard he's been following one of the local girls around. Vicky something or other. Mind you, the way she carries on I'm surprised nothing worse has happened to her.' She paused, unsure whether or not to continue. 'That phone box down there.' She gestured towards the window. 'I've seen Luke in it late at night.'

Dorothy Edwards was not stupid. She, too, seemed to think the telephone calls and the murder might be connected even though the names of the women concerned had not been publicized. Perhaps this was a natural conclusion to draw because both stories had made the front page of the *Rickenham Herald* which covered such a localized area that almost anything was considered worth reporting.

'But you said he had no friends, who would he be ringing?'

'You tell me, Sergeant. And it doesn't seem right of someone his age not to have a few mates. As far as I know he doesn't have any hobbies either. Heaven knows what he does with himself in that flat for hours on end.'

'One more question, would you happen to have seen him on Tuesday evening or night?'

She bent her head to one side as she considered the question. The lines on her face seemed deeper. 'Myra was on late shifts last week. I heard her go out. Later on Luke went out. Of course, I can't swear it was him, but I heard the door close about seven thirty. An hour after that Myra came home. She stopped in to see me for a few minutes.'

'Did you hear Luke come back?'

'No. But that doesn't mean anything, I usually go to bed about nine and I listen to the radio through earplugs to cut out all the other noises.'

'Thank you, Mrs Edwards, you've been very helpful.' And she had. There were no solid facts but she had confirmed what Mrs Johnson had told them. Luke was a loner, Luke spent a lot of time in the public telephone box, Luke had gone out on Tuesday evening and, according to his mother, had not returned until late. It would be interesting to learn where he had been on Saturday when Helen Potter's phone had rung but no message had been left.

He had been in the King's Head.

Having discovered very little from those residents of Magnolia House who were at home, Greg and Eddie had driven the two hundred yards to the pub which served the

134

estate where the car would be marginally safer in its car-park. The King's Head was a one-storey, sprawling build-ing built at the same time as the flats which surrounded it. There was a newish blue and white carpet on the floor and plenty of panelled woodwork. In the shorter side of the L shape of the bar was a space for dancing or karaoke or whatever else the clientele considered to constitute entertainment.

It was too early to be busy. The landlord was slicing a lemon as they entered. He served them and took their money. Unlike the old days it was frowned upon for CID members to drink whilst on duty but it was almost lunch-time and one pint wouldn't hurt.

The place was surprisingly clean. Bottles and glasses sparkled and there were no rips in the upholstery.

'I won't put up with trouble,' the landlord informed them once they had made themselves known to him. 'Can't afford to, not somewhere like this. Where else would my customers come from? Once it starts it gets worse. You get a reputation and then there's no stopping it.'

Ex-forces, Greg guessed, and able to take care of himself, and sensible enough to know what he was doing. 'Do you know Luke Johnson?'

'Yes. I make a point of knowing all my customers. Most of them live round here, we get very few strangers.'

'When did you last see him?'

'Saturday night.'

The answer came quickly; too quickly? 'Can you be certain of that?' Eddie said.

'Absolutely. He's not much of a drinker but he always comes in on Saturdays. He just sits there watching the dancing, one young lady in particular, not that he'll get anywhere with Vicky. Now and then he comes in when there's a darts match. He doesn't play but he'll watch.'

'What time did he leave on Saturday?'

'Same time as most of the others. Eleven thirty when the

music finished. We've got a permanent extension. He always brings his glass back to the bar.'

'Is there a telephone here?'

'Yes. Do you want to use it?' The landlord was reaching beneath the bar.

'A public one?'

'It's in the corridor at the back near the toilets.'

'So if he'd made a call you wouldn't have been able to see him.'

The landlord laughed. 'If you were here on a Saturday night you'd know I wouldn't have time to do more than keep the drinks coming. Sorry, I can't help you there.'

'Can you hear the music from the corridor?'

'The way my customers like it you can probably hear it in Saxborough.'

They left then. It seemed unlikely Luke had made the call, unless he had left the pub to do so. Whoever had rung Helen Potter had not spoken but nor had there been any background noises, only the sound of someone breathing, during those six seconds or so before the receiver had been replaced. They had now replayed the tape but it held no clues.

They saw Brenda pull up outside Magnolia House and stopped the car. 'We've done them all,' Eddie Roberts told her. 'We might as well get back.'

Having relayed his conversation with Mrs Edwards to the rest of the team, Greg Grant sat back in his chair knowing how disappointed they were; no facts, no proof, no names, just the general observations of an elderly lady. 'Did you get anywhere with Jim Hurst?' he asked Alan Campbell, hoping that one of them had good news.

'No. It looks as though he's straight.'

Brenda leaned against the window sill with her arms folded, subconsciously mimicking the Chief's posture when he was thinking. It was after two o'clock and she had not been able to get hold of Cassandra Maguire. She said as much.

'Perhaps she's in the library,' Ian suggested, 'or out

interviewing people. Give it another hour and try again. She can't be expected to stay at home twenty-four hours a day. If you get no joy by the end of the day, go and see her.' He was aware she had been seen driving away on Saturday night. Presumably, having reached her deadline, she had decided to take a day or two off. It would have been greatly appreciated if she had had the decency to let them know where she could be reached.

Brenda nodded. It was unreasonable of them to expect the woman to stay at home waiting for her daily telephone call, but she was worried. If Cass was going to be away for any length of time surely she would have informed them. She shook her head. All this concern and there was still nothing to suggest that the murder was connected to the telephone calls.

Luke had heard the loud knocking on the doors either side of his flat. He knew it was the police and that they were after him. He would have to do something and he had to act fast. He wished he had never heard of Terry Noble or La Pêche.

Never before had he committed a crime, and this was a serious one. Jo Chan wouldn't talk, he couldn't afford to, and Terry certainly wouldn't. But he, Luke, knew that he wouldn't be able to keep his mouth shut under pressure. Even his mother had managed to drag out of him the fact he'd not paid the television rental. And if he told the truth he would probably be charged with murder. And so would Terry. And what would Terry do to him then?

Luke realized he had two choices: confess and take his chances or get away. He decided on the latter.

Chapter Eleven

Another night had passed. They had reached a hiatus. DC Gibbons had tried Cass Maguire's number several times the previous afternoon and when, by teatime, there was still no reply she had driven over to the maisonette. There was no response when she rang the doorbell, not that she had expected one; Cass's car was nowhere in sight and no one had seen her return.

'Inconsiderate bitch,' she had muttered as she returned to her own car.

'Maybe she took your advice, and has gone to stay with someone,' Short had suggested later.

'Then she ought to have let us know.'

That was yesterday. They had heard nothing since and Brenda was still unable to obtain a reply. She had left several messages in the hope that Cass would pick up her calls, but to no avail.

'Anything doing on that break-in?' Ian asked.

'What? The cold-storage place?' John Short fingered his moustache. 'Nothing.'

The Poplars Business Park was at the bottom end of Rickenham Green. Behind it was a country lane bounded by fields. To one side was the Bradley housing estate, to the other an extension of the lane where it wound back over a tributary of the River Deben into the town. The storage warehouse was at the back against the fence with units either side and therefore ideally situated from the point of view of the thieves. No passer-by could have seen them from the road, not that many people had cause to walk along it.

They had interviewed all the warehouse staff, especially the three who held keys. But security was lax and although the alarm had gone off no one had reported it. Sergeant Grant, soundly asleep, had been unaware of it but surely someone on the Bradley estate must have heard it ringing. But it was the way of the world. The things could ring for hours and it was only when they became a nuisance that anyone bothered to make a phone call. And people generally assumed it was a fault. One of the shops in the High Street had had a sensitive alarm which was set off every time a heavy goods vehicle trundled past. Thankfully that had now been replaced.

For lack of new evidence Ian decided they would start questioning everyone for a second or third time, including the five remaining women.

'But I don't know where Cass is,' Brenda said.

'Then find her.'

'Yes, sir.' She was aware that his short temper was due to frustration rather than anything she had or had not done. Cass had mentioned she had been working on an article which had to be in the post by Monday. Yesterday. Perhaps she had got behind with it and had decided to deliver the manuscript herself. Brenda delved into her large shoulder-bag and produced her notebook, hoping she had been efficient enough to jot down the name of the magazine who had commissioned the article because she could not remember it. It was one of the big glossies, she recalled that much; if all else failed she could ring them all. Which was what she had to do.

'May I speak to the beauty editor?' she asked for the fourth time in succession. Having explained who was calling but without giving any more away, she was finally put through to the one for whom Cassandra Maguire had been writing her article.

'Is something the matter?' There was a hint of panic in the editor's well-modulated voice.

Not knowing how much the woman knew about Cass's private life or if there actually was anything the matter, Brenda did not answer the question. She asked one of her own instead. 'I wondered if you could tell me where Miss Maguire is at the moment?'

'No. No, I'm afraid I can't. I've been trying to ring her this morning, ever since the post arrived, in fact. She promised me an article by today, it's our deadline for next month's publication. Whenever we've used her before her work has been posted well in advance.'

'Are you saying it hasn't come?'

'Yes. Naturally we've got replacement articles we can use in an emergency, but for her not to even let us know it wasn't ready is most unusual.'

'Is there any chance she might bring it to you personally?'

'Well, I suppose so. But why hasn't she rung to say as much?'

Brenda thanked her and suggested they use whatever material they had to hand. There had been no communication with Cassandra since Saturday. Wherever she was she had had plenty of time in which to contact both the police and the magazine or to drive down to London if she didn't trust the postal service. It was possible she had worked late into the night to meet her deadline and ignored the telephone and was now on her way to London, intending to ring Brenda as soon as she had delivered her work. But Brenda didn't think so, she wouldn't have ignored so many messages.

She found Ian in his office. 'I think we've got reasonable cause to break in,' she told him. If they believed someone to be in danger it was not illegal to do so without a search warrant. But if Cass Maguire was in that maisonette she wasn't in danger, she was dead.

'Do it. If she's simply taken off without telling anyone she can hardly complain. At least she'll know how worried we were. Take Alan with you, he'll forget how things work in the real world if he doesn't get away from that computer screen now and again.'

They went in one of the pool cars. Brenda drove with a feeling of dread. Alan sat beside her eating a banana, the skin of which he placed on the dashboard.

The sun was bright through the windscreen. Blossom from cherry trees dropped on to the bonnet of the car as they passed one of the playing fields. It was a beautiful, balmy spring day with a hint of a breeze. Brenda hoped she hadn't overreacted. Cass's car was not outside the building and someone had seen her driving away. Even so they could not take a chance.

Alan led the way up the concrete steps and kept his finger on the shrill bell long enough to have disturbed the whole block. He leaned his forehead against the patterned glass but saw no movement inside.

'It's the only way in,' Brenda commented unnecessarily because that much was obvious. 'Oh, shit.'

They had both realized the same thing at the same time. Cassandra had said the place was safe enough and she was right. A brick would bounce off the double-glazed doors and windows which were fitted with locks all the way around. They would need a key to get in. Brenda cursed herself for not thinking of this earlier.

Alan studied the window to the right of the door. The same dishes were on the worktop, there was no sign that Cass had returned. Nor was there any sign of the double-glazing firm's name or insignia on the glass.

'Next door,' Brenda said. 'Look, they've got the same design.'

She rang that bell and was rewarded when a lady in her fifties answered the door. 'Can I help you?'

Brenda took a deep breath. 'We're police officers,' she began, showing her identity. 'Have you seen your neighbour, Miss Maguire, recently?'

'No. Not since – let me see, Friday night. I saw her coming home around nine. It might've been a bit later. I'm Joan Henderson, by the way.'

141

'Have you seen her leave since, Mrs Henderson?'

'It's Miss. No, I haven't, but I'm mostly in the front during the day. She'd leave by the back in her car.'

'Have you heard anything?'

'I rarely do, she's a very quiet neighbour, and I'm a bit deaf.'

'So you wouldn't know if she's had any visitors since Friday?'

'No. My television's on a bit loud at night. I did ask her once if she could hear it but she said it didn't bother her. Has something happened to her?' she asked belatedly.

'We don't know. We need to get into her flat urgently. Did you employ the same double-glazing people as Miss Maguire?'

'It was the other way around. She saw what a good job they'd done to my place and asked me for their name. It wasn't long after she'd moved in. A month or so later she had hers done to match. I can give you their number. I keep it by the phone in case of an emergency, not that I've ever needed to use it. You can't lock yourself out, you see, you have to turn the key . . .'

'Miss Henderson, this is an emergency, could we have the number, please.'

She invited them in to use her phone but Alan went down to the landing below to use his mobile. They did not want Miss Henderson to overhear their reasons for wanting to get into the place even if it was a false alarm. Brenda kept her talking and admired the plants which grew in pots on either side of her front door. 'The others don't bother, not on our floor, but I suppose they're all too busy working. I miss my garden but this place is much easier to look after.' She nodded in the direction of Brenda's shoulder. 'Your young man's back.'

'Any luck?'

'Yes. Someone's on their way now with a key.'

Brenda frowned. 'They keep duplicates?' She tried to recall if any of the other women had double-glazing.

'I don't know, but they said they could let us in.'

They waited on the landing and within fifteen minutes a man in blue overalls appeared at the top of the steps. 'I was in the van. They got me on the mobile,' he said as he turned his back to them and began fiddling with the door. At last it opened. 'Is that it or will you want me to lock up again?'

'If you could just wait here for a minute, please.' Alan went inside, Brenda close behind him. They knew immediately that Cassandra Maguire was dead. The coffee table had been overturned and there were papers scattered over the carpet. Despite one of the side windows which formed the bay being open an inch or so there was the unmistakable smell of death.

The body lay in the smaller area of the L of the living-room. She wore silk pyjamas and a robe and was sprawled half on the floor, half against a leather armchair. Her hair was spread around her like a dark pillow. She had been strangled. Even so Brenda bent down and felt for a pulse, then shook her head.

Alan speed-dialled a number on his phone while Brenda stood staring down at the lifeless body. Another woman, another wasted life. Would she ever get used to the sadness she felt? And if she did, then what would that make her?

'They're on their way,' Alan told her. 'One of us is to wait here, the other to start questioning the neighbours.'

A house-to-house team would be operational soon but the Chief saw no reason in delaying things. Brenda recalled the Chief's words about Alan and his fixation with the computer. 'You can do the door knocking if you like. I don't mind waiting here.'

Alan told the double-glazing man who was chatting with Miss Henderson that he was free to go. It would be hours before that door would be locked again. With a curious glance into the small hall the man shrugged and left without saying another word.

Brenda knew better than to touch anything. She stood still and took in her surroundings. Everything was just as

143

she had seen it last, apart from those papers on the floor and a dead woman in the corner.

With her hands in her pockets she walked back to the kitchen and stood in the doorway. Cass had had visitors, one at least. On the work surface was the crockery she had just been able to make out through the window. But there were two dinner plates, two glasses, several mugs and some cutlery. There was also a side-plate. Had someone shared a meal with her then killed her? How many domestic disputes had started over a meal or the washing up? But Cass had said she did not have a current boyfriend. Unless she had met someone over the weekend, someone who had intended to murder her from the start and had talked his way into her home. And now it seemed more likely to be a man. Anyone could use a knife but to strangle a very fit young woman was not easy.

Alan returned within a few minutes. Miss Henderson had not been able to add anything to what she had said already and there had been no one in at the other two maisonettes on that floor. He would try downstairs in a minute. 'So where's her car?' he wondered aloud. 'Do we know the number?'

'No.' And they couldn't start digging around amongst her papers until the scene-of-crime team had finished.

Alan had no more luck on the floor below. Only one out of four units was occupied. 'They're all out at work,' William Jenkins told Alan. 'Young, all of them. I'm retired now. This place suits me, I can manage on my own here. The wife died a few years ago, you see.' Alan was finally able to ask him some questions.

'Is she the pretty one with long, dark hair? I see her coming and going occasionally but I don't know anything about her.' But he hadn't seen her at all over the weekend, nor had he noticed any visitors going to the upper floor.

Alan rejoined Brenda. They waited on the landing until the first units drew into the car-park and the various teams arrived. It would be crowded with so many people inside

144

and the scene might look chaotic to an outsider but every member knew exactly what was expected of them.

Brenda went down to their car and radioed through to the station with a request for someone to find out Cass's registration number and to put out an APB on the car. If the murderer had driven it away it should contain evidence. The neighbour might have mistaken the time she had seen it, the car might be in for repairs or perhaps Cass had parked it somewhere else for some reason, but they still needed to find it.

They heard more footsteps and turned to find the Chief standing behind them in the shadow created by the stairwell. His expression was stern. He checked in with the officer who was recording the arrival and departure of all police personnel before turning to Alan and Brenda. 'I was so very much afraid of this,' he said. 'I've arranged for an officer to be with the other four twenty-four hours a day.' Four female officers out of commission, four highly trained officers, but if it saved another life the strain on their resources was worth it. 'I've also contacted Maggie Telford and told her to return to her home. Someone will escort her there after she finishes surgery.'

Brenda and Alan understood the logic. With a policewoman accompanying her she would be safer in her own house than at the hotel where, as she had correctly pointed out, people were coming and going all day.

The pathologist arrived, breathless from climbing the stairs. He greeted Ian and one or two others he knew then went in to examine the body. There was little surprise when he said that death was caused by strangulation. From the marks around the neck and the pin-point haemorrhages in the eyes a layman could probably have ascertained that.

The photographers and video operators completed their task and the scene-of-crime people, in protective clothing, began preparing their equipment for collecting samples. John Cotton was head of the team. He and Ian had known one another for years, and liked each other. John surveyed the room, taking everything in before anything more was touched. 'Okay, let's go,' he said, pulling on latex gloves. He, like his men, was dressed in a regulation non-static coverall. Every minute particle would be removed and bagged, fingerprints would be taken from every surface and then Ian and his team could go through Cassandra Maguire's papers and personal belongings.

'The kitchen – there are two sets of crockery. If she was entertaining someone there're bound to be prints. No one eats dinner with gloves on.'

There was no dishwasher. Cass earned good money but it would have been an unnecessary luxury for a person living alone, especially one who – as she had told Brenda – ate out a lot. But there was a microwave and a small deep freeze.

'We might as well wait downstairs,' Ian suggested.

They waited on the square of lawn at the back of the building. It had narrow borders of flowers and a small tree in the middle. To their left were washing lines, beyond them small sheds with numbers corresponding to those of the maisonettes, and then came the car-park. The area was sheltered and the sun was warm on their heads. A bee flew between two plants, carrying out its business, unaware of the tragedy which had occurred. Life goes on, even among death, Short would have said, Ian thought. And he was right. And it was up to Ian and others who lived to find the person who had killed these women. He reached into his jacket pocket and took out cigarettes. He was far enough away from the crime scene to smoke. It was Alan Campbell who voiced his thoughts.

'I suppose we have to assume it's the same man, sir.'

Assume. How many times had Ian told people that you could and should never assume anything. But in this case the chance of two of the women who had received obscene telephone calls being murdered by two different people seemed extremely remote. On the other hand life was full of coincidences, some of which also defied credibility. And in these two cases the method was different. Julie Watson had been stabbed, Cassandra Maguire was strangled; the former had been killed at a place of work, the latter at home, and the likelihood was that she had fed her killer first. Food. Was there a connection? A restaurant, a meal provided. And the theft of frozen meat. The thought came from nowhere. He pulled out his cell phone. 'I want Matthew Watson, Anthony Smithson, Luke Johnson and Jim Hurst brought in and questioned again. I want to know their every movement between – hold on. When did you last speak to Cass, Brenda?' He turned to face her.

'Saturday. She answered my call at about eleven thirty and everything was fine. Mrs Henderson last saw her on Friday night but another neighbour claims she saw her driving away about nine thirty on Saturday evening.'

'Thanks.' He spoke into the phone. 'Between eleven o'clock Saturday morning and midnight last night.' Just to be on the safe side, he thought. The pathologist had estimated that she had died sometime between Saturday evening and midday Sunday, certainly no later than that. Time of death was one of the most difficult things to establish, so much depended on changes in temperature, whether the body had been moved, whether it had been immersed in water and many other factors. Ian wanted the men to account for the whole weekend. 'And while you're at it, have another go at Schofield and Maggie's ex, Mark Hopkins.' He listened for a few seconds. 'Well, that's something, I suppose.'

He put the phone back in his pocket and looked up. Figures on the balcony were starting to make their way towards the stairs. 'It looks as if we can go in now,' he said, peering around for somewhere to put the cigarette end he had trodden on. 'Eddie Roberts has spoken to the second waitress. She says that Schofield talked to them for about ten minutes or so, had a word with the head chef and left the Grand at quarter past eight. Allowing time for him to get to his car and drive from Saxborough to Rickenham, it would make his arrival time at Maggie's right.' He sighed.

Six possible suspects, it was more than anyone could hope for, but they still hadn't been able to prove a thing.

Luke Johnson had already packed a bag when the knock on the door came. He sank down on the side of his bed, his head in his hands. They know, he thought. His mother would be so ashamed of him. There was no escape, no other way out of the flat than the window and he'd probably break both legs if he chanced it. And he didn't have the heart to run now. He stood, took a deep breath and went to answer the door. It was a relief in a way because he had had no idea where he could go.

Two policemen were in the hall, ready to face violence or for Luke to try to run past them. They saw a man in his late twenties or early thirties wearing jeans, a T-shirt and trainers. It was a young man's summer uniform. His dark hair was cut short and he was good-looking although he would soon be overweight. He wasn't a slob, he had shaved and his clothes were clean. No ear-rings, no visible tattoos. They took it all in quickly.

'You'd better come in,' Luke said.

'We'd like you to come with us to answer a few questions, please.'

'Yes, okay. Can I use the toilet first?'

One of the oldest tricks in the book. But the flats in Magnolia House were designed in such a manner that none of the bathrooms had windows, only extractor fans. They knew this from experience, it was far from their first visit to the place. The other possibility was that Luke Johnson intended to lock himself in and cut his wrists. 'If you keep the door open,' one of the officers told him.

They followed him and waited by the open door while he urinated and washed his hands.

'Were you going somewhere?' The second officer nodded towards the open bedroom doorway. On the floor stood a bulging holdall with the zip done up.

'Yes. I was going away. Can I leave a note for my mother?'

'No. You can ring her later, if necessary.'

Luke walked between them and got into the back of the marked car without further comment. He had the short trip to the police station in which to decide just how much he ought to tell them.

Before Ian had finished listening to the taped interviews of all six men their alibis were being checked. Only the third one was, for the moment, of any interest. DC Eddie Roberts and DS Greg Grant had interviewed Luke Johnson.

'Where were you on Saturday evening from, say, six o'clock onwards?'

'At home. Mum was at work. I made myself something to eat then went to the King's Head.' Ian knew the two detectives already had confirmation of this from the land-lord there.

'What time did you get home?'

'Quarter to twelve. Mum'll tell you that. She never goes to bed early when she's on a late shift.'

'Did you leave the house again?'

'Whatever for? Look, I thought you were going to ask me about the . . .'

'About what?' Greg Grant had wanted to know.

'Nothing.'

Apart from the time he had spent in the pub Luke Johnson had no real alibi for the rest of the weekend. Which, knowing what they did about him, would be nor-mal if he was innocent. However, the officers who had brought him in said he seemed relieved and Luke now gave the impression that he was expecting to be ques-tioned about something else. It was Eddie Roberts who took the chance.

'There's just one more thing, can you recall where you were last Wednesday night?'

That had been enough for Luke. 'Poplars Business Park,' he had blurted out.

'Alone?'

'No.'

'Who with?'

'I don't know his name.'

No, Ian thought, you wouldn't. But they had a confession. Luke Johnson had been one of two people to break in and steal over four thousand pounds' worth of frozen meat. He didn't have the meat. He didn't know where it was. He didn't know why it had been stolen. 'This bloke said we would go halves, that he knew where he could sell it. I don't know any more than that.'

'Have you been paid?'

'No.' But Eddie had told Ian that he was sure Luke was lying, that he was protecting someone. But who and why? And if he was capable of committing one crime, why not another?

It was nearer to eight o'clock than seven, the time Ian had told Moira to expect him, when he reached home. She was in the garden, watering the three-inch high runner beans. Long shadows fell across the grass and the shrubs rustled in the chilly breeze which had sprung up. Ian watched his wife for a few seconds. She had not heard his approach. Bent over the border where he had erected the canes for the beans, the smallness of her waist was accentuated. Her hair had fallen across her face; she flung it back impatiently as she straightened up. 'Ian! I didn't realize you were there.'

He smiled, unable to imagine what his life would be like if he didn't have Moira to come home to each evening. Sometimes he told her how he felt, but perhaps he didn't tell her often enough. Such talk had always embarrassed him and he hoped she knew without him having to repeat it. 'I'm more in need of a drink than the beans are,' he said. 'Can I pour you one?'

'Love one. Thanks. I've almost finished out here now.'

150

She walked down to the small shed and replaced the watering can then joined Ian in the kitchen, closing the door behind her. She shivered, there was gooseflesh on her arms.

'There's been another one,' he said as she pulled on a cardigan.

'Oh, no.' Moira sat at the table opposite him, knowing immediately what he was referring to. 'You were afraid of that, weren't you?'

'Yes. And I keep thinking we could have prevented it.'

'How?'

He told her all that had happened over the weekend. 'We should've insisted she stayed with someone. And then, when she didn't answer the phone, we should've broken in immediately, not taken the word of a neighbour that she'd gone off in the car.'

The latter course of action would not have prevented her death but Moira did not say so. 'Have the others got a police guard, or whatever you call it?'

'Yes. It's the very least we can do.'

Moira got up to see to their meal. Even though she now worked full time she still attended to most of the housework and cooking. Ian, being older than her, had been brought up in a different era when few women went out to work. Because of that and the long-established habits of their marriage, it did not occur to him to help out. But on nights such as this Moira would never have expected him to help, and she had to admit that it didn't really bother her. With the gadgets they had acquired over the years housework was not the chore it had once been. She began to sauté chicken breasts then left them to see to the vegetables.

'Smells good, I hope there's plenty of garlic.'

'There is.'

Food. Again the tenuous connection crossed his mind. The restaurant, the meal Cass had shared with an unknown visitor, and the frozen meat . . .

151

'You said you were going to interview the men again. Did you find out anything new?'

'Not a lot really.' Matthew Watson and his girlfriend, Debbie, had gone to visit her parents in the Midlands. They had left on Saturday morning and returned on Sunday evening. This had been verified by his future in-laws and a neighbour who saw them returning. Jim and Maria Hurst had been in the restaurant from five thirty until well after midnight on Saturday, a fact which had been confirmed by the staff who had also been there, then they had returned home together, exhausted by their first night in business. They had spent the early part of Sunday morning in the garden then Jim had gone in to oversee the Sunday lunches. He'd gone home for an hour or so then returned again for the evening opening. There were gaps, understandably so, but unless his wife was covering for him it seemed unlikely that he'd had enough time to kill Cassandra Maguire.

And Anthony Smithson. He had been totally pissed off at being questioned again. He'd gone into work for an hour or so on Saturday morning then played squash. He had no alibi whatsoever for the rest of the weekend until Sunday evening when he'd called into his local pub where the landlord knew him. He was still a candidate.

Last, but certainly not least, was Luke Johnson. One case partially solved but unless Luke talked that would probably be the end of it.

'It's understandable,' Moira said as she stirred seasoning into the chicken juices in the pan. 'Him protecting his mate. Or perhaps he's afraid of the repercussions if he does talk.'

'He's afraid, all right.' But of whom? His mother? That was doubtful and this was his first offence, his first known offence. Luke was thirty years old, it was a bit late to start a criminal career, unless he had, so far, been particularly successful. No, there weren't that many similar crimes that they hadn't cleared up, if not immediately then when they were taken into consideration on later charges. If Luke was telling the truth about hardly knowing the bloke then it would be wise to see who was new to the area and if they had a record. That would have to wait until tomorrow. For now there was another beer to drink and a delicious-smelling meal to eat.

Chapter Twelve

Pam Richards' feelings were a combination of relief and fear as she stepped inside her front door. Relief that she was back at home but fear that the delicate-looking, fair-haired WPC would be no match for a killer if he decided to come after her. Pam did not know that nowadays, whether male or female, an officer was plain PC, nor was she aware that Camilla Fletcher, unless faced with a gun, was as good as any man. Her looks helped in her work. They stated helplessness and therefore provided an element of surprise when she was thrown into the thick of things.

'It's a lovely cottage,' she said as she walked from room to room, checking doors and windows, checking anything which might leave them vulnerable or which would serve as protection. Pam had been staying with her mother who, since her divorce, lived in a one-bedroomed house. With Pam sleeping on the settee, there was simply no room for one more person. Besides, having the women at home might attract the killer, and they now knew what they were dealing with. Every telephone call would be monitored, no door would be opened except by the officer in the house, and then not immediately, not until the identity of the caller had been verified.

'It is, but I don't know if I'll ever feel safe here again.'

'We'll get him and then you can put it all behind you.'

'No, I don't think so. Two people are dead, people who

look like me and probably had everything to live for. It could've been me.'

'But it wasn't you, Pam, and it won't be. I'll even sleep in the same room as you if you prefer it.'

'Thanks, but that won't be necessary. Shall I make some coffee?'

'Good idea. If you show me where things are we can take it in turns.' Camilla Fletcher knew that Pam was low, almost to the point of depression. She must get her out of it, get her mind concentrated, and then she might be able to remember something useful.

Helen Potter was back in her flat. PC Sally Moorehouse had gone in first. There was nothing out of the ordinary other than a thin film of dust in an otherwise clean and tidy apartment, and the answering-machine was devoid of messages. 'When's your boyfriend back?' she asked once she was satisfied the flat was safe and the door was locked behind them.

'Early next week, thank goodness. If he'd been here I needn't have troubled Jill. God, it's good to be home.'

But by the end of the first evening Helen realized she had simply exchanged one sort of prison for another. And now, to cap it all, the police had said that none of them could go to work, they needed to know exactly where they were at all times. Her sister was fully aware of the circumstances and now that there had been a second murder she was relieved that Helen was under police protection. 'Don't worry, you won't lose out on money, it's a partnership, don't forget. I've already found someone willing to help out temporarily. And I know you'd do the same for me. Stay put for as long as they tell you to. I'll ring every morning and evening to see how you are,' Jill had told her.

Not even to be allowed outside in such lovely weather was a real hardship for Helen who, when the sandwich bar

155

closed at three, spent as many daylight hours as possible out of doors.

Janice King remained with her brother Ben and his wife because they had a four-bedroomed house and the more people who were around, the better. They had no objections at all to the presence of PC Maureen Pearce. In fact, Maureen got the impression that Fliss, Ben's wife, found it rather exciting and a bit of a joke. Time will tell, she thought, as the days wear on we'll probably all be sick of the sight of each other. But Janice seemed happier for having her there.

No work tomorrow, Janice was thinking. She had rarely taken a day off sick and her employer had been understanding, especially when news of the second murder had broken when she must have put two and two together. 'You must do what they say, Janice, you can't take any chances now,' she had said. 'You'll still get your wages at the end of the week although I expect you'll miss your tips. I'll make sure your regulars are looked after.'

So now she must wait, she must stay in the house at all times and not go near the windows if she could avoid it. It all seemed a bit melodramatic until she remembered that two women who resembled her were no longer alive.

'But I've got clients to see.' Maggie Telford's reaction was predictable when it was explained to her that it was better if she returned home in the company of a police officer and did not attend the surgery until further notice.

'The decision is yours, we can't force you,' Brenda had replied, 'but we can take no responsibility if anything happens to you outside of our protection.'

'But he's not going to come bursting in and shoot me whilst I'm drilling someone's teeth.'

'We don't know that, that's why we want you to take these precautions. Julie Watson was at her place of work when she died.'

Yes, Maggie thought, Brenda Gibbons has a point, but Julie was there alone. And she was still convinced that nothing could happen to her, that Anthony Smithson, who had made those calls to her, was nothing to do with the murdered women, that she, Maggie, was the exception because she had known who was on the other end of the line.

Without anything being said, Maggie sensed at once that PC Anna Stevenson was a lesbian. Gay, she reminded herself, which was daft. To her it still meant happy, gleeful, even though someone had once explained it was an acronym for 'good as you'.

Anna Stevenson whistled through her teeth as Maggie led her around the spacious house. She was impressed. 'Don't you find it's too big for you?'

Maggie studied the tall, slender figure with her spiky ginger hair and girlish freckles across the nose. 'No. I'm always happier with lots of space. You can pick which bedroom you like. Oh, my boyfriend's supposed to be seeing me tonight. Will that be a problem?'

'No. As long as he doesn't expect you to go out.' One of the possible suspects. But Anna, like the other female officers, was more than a match for any man. She had already checked with the Chief, who had said yes, let him in if he calls. If he tried anything at least they'd know who their man was.

'Good. Now, with all this time on my hands I can make us all something really good to eat.' Maggie decided it would be fun to prove to Anna and Brian how well she could cook.

By the time Brian Schofield arrived later that evening Maggie and Anna were getting used to one another's company. Brian had brought flowers and wine and was charming with Anna who was polite in return.

After they had eaten they sat in the large lounge. Maggie and Brian drank brandy but Anna refused the offer of alcohol. 'I'm still on duty,' she reminded them. And she needed a clear head. Over the meal they had discussed their respective jobs. 'I know the Grand,' Anna had said. 'I used to live in Saxborough. My partner and I used to go there sometimes for drinks or dinner if we were feeling extravagant.'

'It isn't cheap,' Brian agreed. 'But in this case you do actually get what you pay for. It's a headache making sure of it, though, I can tell you.'

They're a handsome pair, Anna thought. Maggie so dark and sophisticated. Even now when she could relax she was dressed in tailored trousers and a silk blouse. Brian was an inch or so taller than her and as fair as she was dark. His eyes were a shade of green she had not encountered before. She could picture the couple at functions and dinners and walking down the aisle, the envy of everyone. Not that she would ever be doing that herself.

Darkness came. Anna drew all the curtains before switching on the lights. Brian had made no move to leave. If he intended staying the night she was sorry she had chosen the bedroom nearest to Maggie's.

It was nearly midnight when he did go. It was Anna who saw him out, even if it meant depriving him of a goodnight kiss on the doorstep. She locked up, double checked that all the windows were closed, then they went to bed.

Forty minutes later the telephone rang. Both women were immediately alert. Anna ran to Maggie's room and burst in without knocking. Maggie had waited for her arrival before answering.

'Hello?' She smiled, put her hand over the mouthpiece and said, 'It's all right, it's Brian. Thanks, anyway.'

Anna went back to her room. It was a long time before the muffled voice she could hear through the wall became silent.

First thing in the morning all four female officers phoned in to report that the night had passed quietly. It was Wednesday, a week since Julie Watson had been found

158

dead, less than twenty-four hours since the discovery of Cassandra Maguire's body. Two murders within seven days and four women were still in danger. Had Cass received a telephone call before her death? If so, she had not told them of it. And she had let her killer in, therefore she had to have known him, therefore, logically, it had to be someone on her list. They were going through it again. The telephone company were going through her incoming calls but that would take some time and if the killer had rung it was bound to have been from a call box. Dialling 1471 hadn't provided any clues. Pressing 3 to return the last call they were connected to the private line of the beauty editor to whom Brenda had spoken. This tallied with the messages on her answering-machine. There were several from Brenda and the editor and one, timed earlier at ten thirty on Sunday morning, from someone called Caro. Caro's number had been in the small leather-bound book Cass had kept by the phone. 'I was ringing to see if she fancied going out for a pub lunch,' she explained when Greg Grant got through to her. 'We don't see each other very often, we're both too busy.' She had now been interviewed. Shocked and tearful, she had been able to tell them little more than that they were in the same line of work and met up three or four times a year. 'We weren't what you'd call close friends but we always enjoyed seeing each other.' She was unable to name anyone else that Cass might have known.

Ian sat at his desk, his hands linked behind his head, the sun warm on his back. Serial killers often worked to a pattern and, according to psychologists, the length of time between killings tended to shorten. One every two years, maybe, then annually and so on, but two in such a short time was ludicrous. And there was no pattern here, other than the one formed by the women in that they looked alike, were single and lived alone. Yes, even Helen Potter lived alone although she had a steady, long-term boyfriend. So how does our man know this? he asked himself again. And how did he get their phone numbers? That man had known where Julie would be on that fateful Tuesday night and had also known that Cassandra was at home at the weekend. Had he followed them or had they been with him willingly? Was he one step ahead of them? Did he know that the other four had now returned home? If so he would also know that they were no longer alone. But would that stop him? Maybe. But for how long could they provide protection? 'Too many sodding questions,' he muttered as he slumped forward over his desk and began doodling on an internal memo he hadn't bothered to read.

Lunchtime. Well, almost. It was ten to twelve. He walked down to the general office. Only John Short was there, the rest of the team was out dealing with their allocated tasks. 'Fancy a drink, John?'

Short grunted. For once he was staring at a computer screen.

'There just doesn't seem to be a common denominator.'

'I know, but there has to be. Are you coming, or not?'

'Yeah.' He pulled himself out of the chair, took his jacket from the back of it and followed Ian out of the door.

Cassandra's name had been released to the press that morning. Her parents lived in Edinburgh and had been informed the previous night, as had her sister who lived in London. All three were on their way to Rickenham Green.

'Warm, isn't it?' Short said as they walked up the High Street. He was sweating. Ian wondered how he would cope when it was really hot. Short wiped his head with a handkerchief then stuffed it back into his pocket.

They threaded their way between women burdened with pushchairs or shopping, other men in suits and a group of children who should have been in school. 'Naughty, naughty,' Short said before realizing he was talking to himself. Ian was some way behind him, waiting to cross the road to take the alley to the Crown, not carrying on to the Feathers as Short had been doing.

Bob Jones greeted them, surprised to see Ian there at

lunchtime. He knew the police favoured the Feathers, although he couldn't think why. Ian used the Crown when work was over or when he took Moira out for a drink. 'Are you eating?'

'I am,' Short said. 'I've heard about your wife's steak and kidney pie, is it on today?'

'Yes.'

'Good. I'll have that. With chips, please.' He put his hand in his pocket to pay for the meal as Bob wrote down the order.

'For you, Ian?' Bob asked.

'Tuna salad, please.' He handed over three pound coins.

Short pulled a face. He couldn't recall when he had last eaten salad, or if, indeed, he ever had. And as for fruit, he didn't even own a fruit bowl. 'And two pints of bitter.' He paid for them both.

At least when he's not on the Guinness he drinks real ale, Ian thought as they went to find a table. The man has to have some redeeming features.

'This one's a real headache,' Short said, serious for once. 'Let's hope Brenda and Eddie can find something relevant.' They were at Cass's maisonette going through her paperwork and possessions. Alan Campbell and Greg Grant were interviewing everyone on the list she had provided for them. It looked as though repair men could be ruled out as the maisonettes had a management company who were responsible for all exterior repairs and decoration, the grounds and the security lighting. The company owned other blocks of flats in the area. The men it employed worked full time for the company and would not, therefore, have had time to do any jobs for the other five women unless they were moonlighting. The management company had faxed through a list of their employees who would all be seen even though none of the names had appeared on the women's lists.

'Nice drop of ale this.' Short held his glass up to the

window. The beer was perfectly clear and almost amber with the sunlight shining through it.

'I know. It always is. Should we be looking at this from another angle, do you think?'

'Such as?'

'Such as . . . oh, hell, I don't know. I just get the feeling that we're dealing with this arse-about-face.'

'I think we all feel that. What you were saying about a pattern – there is one, I think.'

'Go on.' Ian leaned forward expectantly.

'Julie Watson was in the kitchen of La Pêche, right? She was alone. As we've already surmised, after those calls and her obvious fear it was highly unlikely she left the door unlocked. She let the man in so she had to know him. Maybe not intimately but enough to trust him. The same goes for Cassandra Maguire. She'd be even more careful in her own home, and alone. And if we're right, she cooked him a meal.'

'Which means she did know him intimately.'

'Not necessarily. Might've been a first date.'

'No. Not with the way things were. And surely no one in their right mind invites a stranger home on their first, or even second meeting. But I get your point. We need to speak to the others again. There has to be someone they haven't included, probably because they've forgotten about him or think their contact with him is too negligible to mention.' Ian grinned. 'That's it, isn't it? That's looking at it from another angle. Go after the women, not the suspects. There has to be someone they know, someone they trust, but this someone seems relatively unimportant because no one has mentioned him.' But who? What sort of person would they barely know yet trust enough to open the door to them?

Their food arrived. Feeling fractionally more optimistic, Ian ate his salad as if he was really enjoying it. He had smothered the tuna with mayonnaise before realizing the reason he had ordered it was in deference to his waistline.

Short dug into his pie and chips as if he had not eaten for several days. By one o'clock they were back at the station where they both made a couple of phone calls before setting off to see each of the four women. Ian felt he finally had something to work on. He would take Helen Potter and Maggie Telford, Short was to interview Janice King and Pamela Richards. No need for a female officer to accompany them, the women already had a chaperone in the form of the police officers who were staying with them.

It was not a pleasant feeling returning to the scene of a murder, but it was necessary. Brenda also suspected why she had been chosen to go with Eddie Roberts. She was female, her feminine instincts might provide inspiration when going through Cass's things. The Chief, surprisingly, believed in instinct.

Everything was just as they had left it, apart from the outline on the carpet where the lower part of the body had lain and fingerprint dust on the surfaces. But they were now free to touch anything and everything, which is exactly what they would do.

They started in the bedroom. A full-length wardrobe lined one wall, the doors were mirrored glass. Brenda slid it open. There were clothes of every description. It took some time to go through pockets but Cass had been neat and clean. There wasn't so much as a used tissue. Boxes stored on the top shelves held an assortment of old theatre programmes and school reports. They sifted through them anyway.

The dressing-table drawers held underwear, a half-used strip of birth control pills, face creams and very little make-up, the bedside table only a lamp, an alarm clock and a battered paperback.

There was nothing of interest in the tiny kitchen. The crockery had been taken away for further analysis, to ascertain that both plates had held the same food. It had looked that way from the smears of grease and the remains of vegetables. The freezer contained nothing more than frozen food.

The contents of the bathroom were predictable, Cass's only medication was aspirin and a bottle of TCP. That left the living-room, which they had saved until the end because it seemed to be where she kept all her paperwork and where her computer was housed.

Brenda, in jeans and a short-sleeved cotton blouse, bent down to retrieve the papers from the floor. Her hair was loose around her shoulders. The sunlight streaming through the window turned it more auburn than copper. 'This isn't her article, this was the research she was working on,' she told Eddie who had switched on the computer. They were both dressed for summer although it was still only spring. He was also wearing a short-sleeved shirt worn loose over beige chinos.

'I think this is it.' He picked up a small, padded manilla envelope addressed to the magazine editor to whom Brenda had spoken. He opened it and pulled out a computer disk and the accompanying letter. 'Whatever's on here won't ever get published now,' he said sadly, recalling some letters his mother had written on the eve of her death which no one had had the heart to post.

When they left they took away the disk which bore the names and addresses and telephone numbers of all Cassandra's business contacts. They were numerous. None was based in Rickenham Green but she had worked in the cosmetics industry and cosmetics was a link between females.

The forensic team had found the house keys plus a spare set, but there was only one car key which had been in a bowl on a shelf. Brenda, house keys in hand, was about to lock the door behind them when she stopped.

'What is it?'

'These maisonettes, they're on water meters. Well, we know this one is.' In a box file they had discovered paid bills clipped together.

'So?'

'So I've just remembered something.' She went back inside. Eddie followed her, scratching his head beneath his floppy brown hair, a puzzled frown bisecting his forehead.

In the kitchen she took the lid off the swing-bin which they had already gone through. 'I know she was earning good money but perhaps she was environmentally conscientious. Perhaps she didn't have someone here for dinner.'

'I still don't see what you're getting at.'

'Why waste a bowl of water for one plate etc? Maybe she waited until there were enough dishes before washing up.'

Eddie shook his head. 'You've lost me.'

Rummaging through the bin she finally found what she was looking for. 'You see?' she said as she stood and smiled and offered him a waxed carton stained with tea.

It was a couple of seconds before Eddie nodded. 'You think that the plates looked as though they had contained the same meal because they had, but you think she ate them both, one on Friday and another on Saturday.'

'You've got it.'

The box, which had held two chicken Kievs, did not have the limp texture of having been in the freezer. The eat-by date was that of last Saturday. That's what had stuck in Brenda's mind because it was the date of Cass's death. And there was a reduced price sticker on the front. 'She told me how much she disliked cooking. I think she was lazy enough to buy this, eat one then have the second the following night. I've done it myself.' In those early days after she had chucked Harry out, when life had seemed futile and food was only for fuel and not enjoyment. 'That's what was puzzling me. After what she told me I couldn't see her entertaining anyone unless it was someone she knew really well, someone who knew what to expect in the way of food.'

'She might have known her killer well.'

Brenda shook her head. 'I just don't think she did, not if we can't trace him through her list.' More and more of her contacts had been cleared. 'Besides, she also said she went to restaurants to entertain. And she didn't strike me as the sort of person who'd let anyone know she was incompetent in the kitchen. No, Cass wouldn't have served up something like this for a visitor. We'll have to wait for the results but I'll bet we'll find there are no other prints on the plates but hers.'

'If you're right, then we're back to square one. But she let him in, Brenda, and she's got a chain on the door, a proper, secure one which hasn't been broken or damaged in any way.'

They went back outside. The scent of wallflowers was in the air. Eddie didn't seem to notice. 'So just who do you let in when you're already frightened and it's someone you don't know?'

'Apart from the obvious, a genuine meter man or the police, no one. And even a genuine meter man would not gain admittance on a Saturday night.'

Eddie sighed. 'Let's get back. I'd like to see something of my children tonight. They always seem to be in bed by the time I get home lately.'

Brenda sat in the passenger seat. Behind her was a carrier bag containing the computer disk and Cass's desk diary. There were also two other diaries which covered the previous two years. In the back of each one was a list of telephone numbers, some of which had not been transferred forward. Maybe her connection with her murderer stemmed from the past, maybe Julie's did, too. And maybe they would catch this man before he killed again.

Chapter Thirteen

Luke Johnson began to realize how serious the situation was when he learned he was not to be released on bail. Apart from having admitted his guilt, there was no one to put it up for him. He was put on remand, awaiting sentencing. Things might go easier for him if he dropped Terry Noble in it, but Terry would get at him in some way, he was sure to have contacts inside as well as outside prison. And there was that other matter. It was better to keep quiet about that than to go on trial for murder, which is what he was convinced would happen if he talked.

At least his mother had not been as shocked as he had feared. Disappointed, yes, very much so, but she had taken it in her stride just as she had all the other hardships in her life. And it was partly for her he had done it although she would never believe that now.

Ian pulled up outside Helen Potter's building. He had rung to say he was on his way but even so PC Sally Moorehouse would not admit him until she was certain who was on the other side of the door. He had felt foolishly embarrassed when, at her request, he had had to show as much as she could see of his face through the letter-box.

The flat was one of four in a house conversion in Saxborough Road. One of the better conversions, unlike the majority where the rooms were small, the walls were thin, the rents were cheap and the inhabitants were transient. Sally led him along the wood block flooring of the long narrow hallway and into a room with large windows and a high ceiling. Here, too, the floor was wooden with a large Oriental rug in the centre. The settee and armchairs had pale wooden arms and legs and were covered in tan hessian. Minimalist, Ian thought, a touch Scandinavian, but it works. There were splashes of colour amongst the wood tones by way of three huge ceramic pots which rested on the floor. The sandwich business must be profitable for her to be able to afford such a place. He knew from Brenda that she was buying it.

'You know why I'm here,' Ian said when they were all seated.

Helen nodded. Her dark hair looked a little lank that day and there were greyish shadows beneath her eyes. 'Yes. And I've gone through everything. We both have.' She glanced across at Sally Moorehouse. 'Every piece of paper, everything. We've turned the place upside down. We even resorted to word games but I can't come up with another single name.'

'The thing is, the person we're looking for is probably someone you've forgotten about. For instance, have you ever had a pizza or anything delivered?' Most places required a telephone number before delivering. Ian was still thinking along the lines of food.

She shook her head. 'No. Nothing like that. I'm not into ethnic food and if I eat pizza I go out for it.'

'Groceries, furniture, anything?'

Again she shook her head. 'When I moved in my boyfriend, Darren, hired a van and we collected everything ourselves.'

Ian could understand that. If the rest of the flat was as sparsely furnished it would not have taken much effort. And, of course, a lot of modern furniture came in flat packs. 'Flowers?'

'Yes. Birthdays, sometimes.'

An impossible question, but he had to ask. 'I don't

suppose you can recall the florist?' There were three in Rickenham who delivered.

'No. They might have been different each time anyway.'

'When did you receive the last ones?'

'Just after Christmas. They were from my mother. I had flu and she thought they'd cheer me up. And in case you're wondering, they were delivered by a woman. I answered the door in my nightclothes and she sympathized with me because she'd not long got over it herself.'

Despite the negative answer they would check out the florists. Surely the other five, equally attractive women would have received flowers at some point. And florists kept records. Ian remembered only too well another case where a florist's driver had been convicted of murder. He, however, was still inside. Ian brought the conversation around to more general topics. Discussing Helen's life might jog her memory. 'Tell me about your day, what would you usually do?'

'Before all this I used to get to work at about seven thirty and Jill and I would prepare the fillings and be there for the bread delivery. You'd be amazed how many people buy something to eat on the way to work. A bit like the Americans do. That's why we've started buying in muffins and things.

'Anyway, we're usually flat out until about two then it quietens down. We start clearing up then but we still get the odd last minute customer.'

'You shut at three?'

'Yes. Most days I walk or sit in the park before I come home.'

'Do you ever talk to anyone whilst you're there?'

'No. When you've been talking to people since early in the morning it's the last thing you need. It's my breathing space.

'When Darren's here we see each other almost every night. Mostly we stay in, here or at his place, because we're saving to buy somewhere together. He's away a lot at the moment so he mostly stays with his mother. He won't move in here and he doesn't want me to sell until he has an equal amount to invest.'

'And when you do go out?'

'Oh, mostly we go to the cinema or have a meal somewhere. Pizza or pasta usually because the decent restaurants are a bit dear and Darren always insists upon paying.'

'What does he do?'

'He qualified as a design engineer and he's got a permanent job to go to in September but he's taken a year out to work as an aid volunteer wherever aid is needed. He's in Africa at the moment.'

Such a person did not sound like a serial killer but they had slipped up. They had not checked to see if Darren was actually out of the country. Ian asked for his surname and the name of the charity for which he was working, hoping he had made the question sound casual. He glanced at his watch. It was time to call on Maggie Telford.

Maggie and Anna Stevenson would have been unlikely to socialize unless, as now, it was essential. Not only was there a contrast in their appearance but also in their characters and their lifestyles. When Ian arrived he was surprised to see that they had been sitting at the dining-room table playing Scrabble.

Maggie rose to greet him. 'I know it hardly fits in with my image,' she said, gesturing towards the letter-filled board, 'but we've got to do something to pass the time. Can we really not go out?'

'Not for the moment.' She was the coolest of the lot and the least concerned for her own welfare. Even now she was beautifully dressed and made up and seemed to have forgotten that the last time they had met she had admitted lying to the police. He went through the same routine as he had done with Helen and with the same negative result.

Having noticed the vase of flowers, he asked where they came from and if they had been delivered.

'No. Brian brought them with him last night.'

'How long have you known Mr Schofield?'

'About four or five weeks.' She smiled. 'It was one of those chance meetings. I was in the George having a quick drink after a trying day when he knocked into my table and spilled my drink. He offered to buy me another one, we got talking and it went on from there.'

Ian decided to have a quiet word with Anna later. She had met the man, her opinion would be useful. 'And having met him you decided you wanted nothing more to do with Anthony Smithson.'

'Yes.' Her face reddened at the reminder of what she had done.

'Keep thinking, Miss Telford. If you recall anything tell Anna at once.'

Ian left and drove back to the station. John Short arrived almost simultaneously. Short had been no more successful than Ian.

At four thirty the whole team was back at the station. Brenda voiced her theory about the two plates and identical meals which the lab would either prove or disprove if the cutlery yielded other prints than Cassandra's. Yet common sense told Ian that even a killer who had acted in panic would have the sense to get rid of his fingerprints.

When Brenda and Eddie returned with the disk and diaries Alan Campbell had contacted the editors of the magazines for whom Cass had worked. 'They all said much the same thing, that she was reliable, they liked her work but they didn't really know her. Two of them hadn't even met her, the rest had met her only once or twice, lunch with the editor type meetings, out of politeness. No one knew anything about her personal life and, as you would expect, all the beauty editors were female.'

Another dead end, another wasted day. Luke Johnson was under arrest, would the killing stop now? Ian doubted it. He would have bet money that Luke did not know these women. He did know something, though, something he was not prepared to disclose.

'I'm going to see the Super.' Ian left the room. Maybe

they had got it wrong, maybe they ought not to have put an officer in the homes of these women. It might have been better to send them home alone and have the house, rather than the person, under surveillance. Which would have meant two officers for each of them, one to watch the back and another the front. But resources wouldn't stretch that far.

He stomped up the stairs. Helen Potter's boyfriend was in the clear. The aid charity he worked for had confirmed he was in Africa and due to return home within a week. Investigation into Brian Schofield's background threw up nothing sinister. He had been in the hotel business since he left school. Ian had spoken to one of the members of the board who owned the group of hotels of which the Grand was one. 'We wouldn't want to lose him,' he had said. 'He came with glowing references and he's lived up to them. If he ever fancies a change we wouldn't hesitate to offer him another of our hotels.'

'I don't know, Ian,' Superintendent Mike Thorne said when he'd suggested swapping to external surveillance. 'It's a bit cat and mouse. If he knows the women are being guarded he's unlikely to make a move, although we can't keep them prisoners in their own homes for ever. If we have men outside there's always a chance he'll get by them. Besides, we couldn't keep that up for long.'

Ian understood the problem. It was not easy keeping somewhere under surveillance and extra activity in the suburban areas in which the women lived would not go unnoticed. In Maggie's case there was a park opposite. The only way to watch the front was to have someone in a car, which was far too obvious.

'Have Cass's parents arrived?'

'Yes. They flew to Heathrow and drove up in a hired car. The sister's here, too.'

Thorne sat back and stared at the ceiling as he tried to find a solution. 'It's stalemate at the moment but if he's true to form he'll only be able to wait a limited amount of time. He'll get frustrated and make a mistake. There's been no response from the general public so what I think we'll do is this. We'll pick one of the women and do as you suggest, have the PC removed and the house watched instead. You know them. Decide who's likely to be the strongest and take into consideration surveillance opportunities. Let me know when you've got it arranged.'

Ian went back downstairs. Without doubt Maggie Telford was the strongest and the most likely to co-operate but her house was the biggest problem. Pam Richards was scared and her cottage was out of the question. Surrounded only by fields there was nowhere anyone could watch it unobserved. Which left Janice King and Helen Potter, both of whom lived in flats. Helen's was on the Saxborough Road, which was a busy thoroughfare. There was lots of pedestrian activity because of the numerous flats and shops in the vicinity so it was a possibility. Janice King was still at her brother's. Ian needed to check where she lived and if the position was better they would ask her if she was willing to return home.

'64b High Street, over the greengrocer's', Brenda replied in answer to Ian's question.

'You've been there. What's the layout like?'

'There's a door from the street which opens on to the stairs. There's another door at the top of the stairs which is the entrance to the flat. There's one bedroom which looks out over the yard at the back, living-room at the front and a small kitchen and bathroom. Other than via the bedroom or bathroom windows there's no access from the back to the flat itself, only to the shop below.'

'What's directly opposite?' Ian tried to picture the High Street but failed to recall which shop stood where.

'Lavender's chemist and a Clark's shoe shop. I don't know which exactly.'

'Check them out. See if there's living accommodation above or just storage space. Now, let's see if Janice is prepared to take the risk and if either leaseholder of those establishments is willing to co-operate. If not we'll have to arrange something else.' It would be easy to have people placed in the busy High Street as long as they changed them regularly. People posing as shoppers or window cleaners or gas men digging up the road. 'Now, I need someone to go and speak to Janice again.'

Scruffy Short glanced at his watch. He was picking Nancy up at seven. There was nothing to go home for first so he volunteered.

'Ring me at home and let me know what she says,' Ian told him. 'Meanwhile I want someone to go to the High Street.' It was five past five. There was just time before the shops shut. This time it was Alan who volunteered. Brenda sighed with relief. She could have a whole evening with Andrew.

'That's it. I'll be at home if you want me,' Ian concluded.

And so will I, Eddie Roberts thought with the knowledge that he would be there in time to bath his children, a pleasure he was rarely able to indulge in. He thoroughly enjoyed fatherhood and liked to take his small son and daughter out whenever he had the opportunity.

Greg Grant was ashamed for feeling grateful that the two murders had distracted him from his own grief. But tonight he must return to his empty house with the whole evening ahead of him. He could ring his daughter, of course, but he tried to keep his calls to a minimum. It was not fair on her or her new marriage to burden her, not that she seemed to mind. And it's time I found a hobby, he decided as he put on his suit jacket prior to leaving. He always had and always would wear a suit to work. There was a bit of garden at the back of the house, maybe he could make something of that and, as many people had told him, there were clubs and classes he could attend. No, he needed something he could do alone. A bit like Julie Watson, he had never been one for joining things. He would sit down and give it some thought that evening.

Short plodded out of the building and got into his car. Allowing for teatime traffic it was a twenty-minute drive to the road where Janice King's brother and his wife lived in their four-bedroomed detached house. White clouds were gathering and, as they passed across the sun, buildings were thrown into shadow. The feathers of the pigeons on a rooftop were ruffled by the breeze. Short, thinking of Nancy, was oblivious to everything else. He drove automatically, stopping at traffic lights and pedestrian crossings and indicating whenever necessary. He pulled into the drive in Deben Close surprised to find himself there so quickly.

Benjamin King, some years older than his sister, had done well for himself. According to Brenda, he and his wife were in their early forties. There were no children, but whether this was from choice or because of medical reasons she did not know. Short had rung to say he was on his way.

PC Maureen Pearce opened the door. She stepped backwards to let him in. 'There're all in the lounge, sir.' She indicated a door to her left.

'Inspector Short,' she announced when she had shown him in.

Fliss King stood up then sat down again. She had been expecting someone who looked more like her idea of a detective, not the dishevelled, none-too-clean plump man with the thinning hair who stood grinning at the room in general.

Maureen completed the introductions then sat down.

'We don't mind Janice staying here for as long as is necessary, do we, Fliss?' Ben King said. He, too, was a bit startled by the unprepossessing Inspector.

'That's what I'm here to talk about. Would you like to go home, Janice?'

'Of course I would. I mean, I like staying here but it isn't fair to Ben and Fliss and I miss the flat. Daft, isn't it, but I enjoy watching the activity in the High Street knowing no one can see me.'

'The thing is, as you know, the other women have gone home and they're . . .'

'And Maureen would come with me?' Janice frowned. 'There really isn't the room.'

'We know that.' He paused, wondering how long it would be before someone caught on to what he was suggesting. It was Fliss who did so.

'Are you saying you expect Janice to be on her own when you haven't caught that man yet?'

'Not exactly. What we intended was for Janice to go home and we would have someone watching the flat twenty-four hours a day.'

'That's all very well, but if he got in your people might not get there in time.'

There is that, Short thought. If someone was watching from across the street they'd have to run downstairs, cross the road, get through a door which might be locked, go up the staircase and hope the flat door was open. Okay, they'd catch their killer but, meanwhile, another woman might die. 'The choice is yours, Janice. If you did this, and it would only be on the condition that we're certain we can have men in place, you would be doing us and the public a great service.' He was not aware how pompous he sounded.

'What about food?'

Maggie Telford apparently had a freezer well stocked with meat, fish and vegetables, Pam Richards, because of her distance from any shops, likewise and Helen Potter had arranged for her sister Jill to shop for her whenever necessary. However, this was different. Janice wasn't going to like this bit. 'You can go shopping. We want you to act as normally as possible. You won't see them, but some-one'll be with you the whole time.'

'Can I go back to work?'

'No. It would be too difficult to keep an eye on you there. Our men wouldn't be able to tell who was a customer or who wasn't.

'Do you need time to think about it?' Short studied her and hoped his face didn't betray what he was thinking. Her jeans were skintight over slender legs and she wasn't wearing a bra beneath her T-shirt. Now it was cooler her nipples were visible. He shifted in his chair. Thank goodness he was seeing Nancy tonight.

'I'll do it,' she said. 'If it means an end to it all, I don't mind you using me as bait.'

Well observed, my girl, Short thought. That's exactly what we are doing but we didn't intend for you to know that.

She stood up but Short held up a hand. 'Not so fast. We have to get people in place before we can dream of letting you go. It won't be tonight. Just carry on as before until someone gets in touch with you. If it's convenient maybe your brother could take you home. We don't want to arouse suspicion by using one of our officers.'

Janice sat down again. She was half frightened, half excited at what might lie ahead.

Maureen showed Short to the door. 'Tasty,' he whispered as he inclined his head in the direction of the lounge.

Maureen appeared not to have heard him but she shut the door with more force than was necessary.

Alan Campbell walked to the High Street because although driving would have taken only a couple of minutes there was nowhere to park. With his long stride it took him less than ten minutes. Without seeming to, he looked over and up at the windows of 64b. Neither the chemist's nor the shoe shop was directly opposite but both had upstairs windows from which the front door could easily be seen.

The man behind the dispensary counter was the leasehold owner of the property. About fifty years old, he was lean and tanned. His thick, springy hair was completely white. Bifocal glasses were perched on his nose in a way which suggested he wasn't yet used to them. Alan asked if he could speak to him privately.

'Of course.' He told the girl at the other counter that he'd be back in a few minutes then led Alan into a small kitchen with tea-making facilities and a table-top fridge.

Once Alan had explained the situation, but not the reason why they needed to watch the premises opposite, the man, whose name was indeed Lavender, Hugh Lavender, agreed to the request. 'It's only a storeroom,' he said. 'I let it out once but I had nothing but trouble from the tenants and the business does well enough, even in this day and age, so I haven't bothered since. Do you want to have a look?'

'If I may.'

Alan followed him through the dispensary, through a fire door which was double-locked for security reasons, out of another locked door into the alley behind the building. They ascended a metal fire escape. Lavender unlocked the door and let them in. The place smelled of soap and toiletries, and boxes were stacked around the walls. The main room was completely bare except for a new-looking carpet on the floor. There were no curtains at the windows. 'My tenants took them with them,' Lavender explained with a shrug.

Alan nodded. It didn't matter. He stepped across to the window and looked down into the street. It was ideal. He could also see into Janice's window, or would have been able to if it was dark and she had a light on. As it was, the angle of the sun, which had appeared between clouds, made it impossible to see anything other than blank glass. 'I have to ask that you keep this entirely to yourself.'

'Of course. I won't even tell my wife. You have my word on that.'

The powers that be will be pleased, Alan thought, once the final arrangements had been made. Lavender had refused remuneration for any inconvenience.

'Call it my good citizen's contribution,' he had said. 'It's not as if I live there. Oh, will it be all right to come up for goods if we need to restock the shelves?'

'Yes, act as if nothing is different, but you'll have to

come yourself, your assistant mustn't know. We hope this won't be for more than a couple of days.'

Ian was watching the local news programme when Short rang to say that Janice had agreed to go home. A few minutes later Alan confirmed that the chemist had agreed to allow them to use his premises for surveillance.

Ian put down the phone and rubbed his hands together, an unconscious action he performed when he believed they were getting somewhere. The trap was set, or would be in the morning. The killer would come to them now, Ian was sure of that.

By eight thirty the following morning two men were in place in the bare room above Lavender's. Two because, as conscientious as a man might be, it was easy enough to lose concentration for long enough for someone to have opened that door. They had equipment with them, a camera with a zoom lens and a telescope through which they could see into Janice's flat.

Armed with flasks and sandwiches they settled down to wait. Janice should be arriving sometime soon. Her brother had taken an hour or so off work in order to be able to drive her home and make sure she was safely in the flat.

It had already been ascertained that the relief of the two men should prove to be no problem. There were three entrances to the alley, one at either end and one in the middle, leading from a car-park. They and their replacements could come and go from various directions without attracting undue attention. On the off-chance that anyone did notice, the chemist was to say that he had acquired new tenants.

At nine forty the men noted that Janice King and her brother had entered the door. They had been given photographs to make sure there was no mistake. At nine fifty-eight Ben King reappeared in the street. Janice's face appeared in the window but she did not look in their direction. As far as she knew the flat above the chemist's was empty. There were still no curtains, nothing had altered. She imagined there would be men down in the street and was looking to see if she could pick them out.

Ten minutes later she disappeared into another room and the men continued their observation of the street door.

Chapter Fourteen

Now that steps had been taken to draw the killer in, Ian began to feel more positive. It was just a case of waiting. Janice King might not be the next one on the man's list but she was the only one now available to him. He finished shaving and went downstairs.

Moira was about to leave for work. Over a tight-fitting grey skirt she wore a thin cream boat-neck jumper. As she was short and slender plain clothes suited her best. It had rained heavily in the night and was still drizzling. She kissed the top of Ian's head as he sat down, a mug of tea in his hand. He had slept later than normal, feeling that he deserved a break. 'See you later,' she said, picking up her umbrella.

'I'll ring if I'm going to be late.'

She smiled. 'I know. I'm luckier than some, you always do.' She left by the front door, collecting her raincoat from one of the pegs in the hall before she did so.

Ian finished the tea, rinsed his mug in the sink, checked his hair in the mirror that was perched on top of the upright fridge/freezer then went to retrieve his car keys from the hall table where Moira, some years previously, had insisted he leave them to save the endless searches involving them both when he couldn't remember where he'd put them. He was the same with everything at home but he now had a system which had become an ingrained habit.

In the car he flicked the wipers to clear the drops of water which still clung to the windscreen then headed towards the town centre. Last night, after hearing from Short and Alan Campbell, Ian had rung Anna Stevenson on her mobile phone and asked what she had thought of Brian Schofield. 'Don't answer if Maggie's within earshot,' he had added.

'She's in the bath. He's extremely good-looking, polite and intelligent, and he obviously thinks the world of Maggie. He's been married but it didn't work out. His wife ran off and left him. He might be a good actor, though, and it's hard to say on such a brief acquaintanceship – and, of course, the situation wasn't natural. It wasn't as if I'd been introduced as a friend or anything.'

'Could he have done it? No, don't answer that.' Ian had realized it was a ridiculous question. There wasn't a person, living or dead, who, given the right circumstances, wasn't capable of murder. Moira had once told him that if anything happened to Mark, even as an adult, she wouldn't hesitate to kill the person responsible if it was possible to get at them, without regard to the consequences.

'The thing is, sir,' Anna had continued, 'they'd planned to go away this weekend. They've booked a hotel in the Lake District and they want to know if they can still go. Maggie only mentioned it after you'd left. It's not that often Brian can get a long weekend off.'

Anna had sounded sympathetic. Living under police protection was hardly a good start for a new romance. 'I'll think about it,' he had said. 'I'll let her know by lunchtime tomorrow.' The Lake District, he thought as he put down the phone. Where Jim Hurst had come from. Was there any connection between the two men? Were they in it together? Or was this, as was so often the case, another coincidence?

Ian had not forgotten his promise of the previous night. He discussed it with Superintendent Thorne rather than take the full responsibility. 'I don't see why not, as long as you speak to him first,' he said after giving it some thought. 'If it is Schofield he isn't going to make it obvious by harming her when we know exactly where she is and who she's with. But I can't see it. His alibis for both occasions are watertight.'

On the night of Julie Watson's murder Brian had had dinner with Maggie and had then stayed the night. Schofield had said as much himself and the staff at the hotel bore out his story about a dispute. When Cassandra Maguire had been killed he had been on duty at the hotel. At the end of a long, tiring day he had had a late night drink with Maggie who was staying there at the time. This had all been corroborated. 'I'll let them know, sir, and I'll speak to Schofield right away.'

In his office Ian got the switchboard to put him through to the Grand Hotel in Saxborough. Then he waited while Schofield was paged to come to the phone.

'What can I do for you, Chief Inspector?' Schofield said.

'I believe you and Maggie have plans to go away for the weekend.'

'We do. Is there any chance we still can?'

'Yes, but only if you follow our instructions to the letter.'

'Certainly. Just tell me what they are. It'll do her good to get away from all this for a while.'

'I take it you intend driving.'

'It would take too long to get there by any other means.'

'What time were you thinking of setting off?'

'Lunchtime tomorrow, about twelve. I've got a few things to see to before I can leave.'

'All right, what we'll do is this. Anna Stevenson and another officer will bring Maggie to the hotel. If you can be ready in your car you can go straight off.'

'Is there any chance someone will be following?'

'We can't guarantee there won't be, but it's unlikely.' The only way that could happen was for the murderer to be conveniently sitting outside Maggie's house in a car. 'When are you due back?'

'Sunday night because we assumed Maggie would be at work on Monday morning. But I've got Monday off so perhaps we could stay an extra night.'

It would be one less person to worry about for a night or so. 'That's fine. We'll need to know where you're staying, just as a precaution, and we'd like you to follow the same routine, in reverse, upon your return.'

'Anything to keep her safe. Thanks. You don't know how much I've looked forward to this break.'

Ian hung up then dialled the number of the hotel where Schofield and Maggie would be staying. Satisfied that a room had been booked in their name he replaced the receiver, wondering if they had made a mistake, if, maybe, Schofield had no intention of taking her there. No, not even a desperate man would be that foolish.

On Ian' s desk was a report covering the interview with Cassandra Maguire's parents and sister. He had only read half of it when the telephone rang. It was PC Camilla Fletcher.

'Pamela Richards has just received another call, sir. Can you send someone over to collect the tape?'

'Hold on.' Ian picked up another receiver and issued instructions. 'What did he say?'

'Not much. There wasn't enough time for the call to be traced. He just said, "You're next."'

'Okay. Stay put and be extra careful.' He sat without moving for several minutes. Now was the time to have a known police presence at Pam's cottage but he had to weigh things up. There was a balance somewhere between endangering her life and catching the killer. And if he had rung again it seemed likely he didn't know there was a policewoman in the house. But something was wrong. That call did not fit the pattern. No threat had been issued to the two dead women, they had had no warning whatsoever. Why change now? The answer was obvious. To divert attention away from his intended victim who, logically, had to be Janice King. He does know, Ian thought, he knows that he can't get to the other three. He's been

184

watching and waiting all the time. A surge of optimism flooded through him. It wouldn't be long now and it would be over. But to be on the safe side he would have an unmarked car parked as inconspicuously but as near as possible to Pamela Richards' cottage.

Luke Johnson soon realized he was not suited to captivity. Sitting in the flat all day was quite a different matter from being under lock and key. He wanted out and he would take his chances with Terry Noble. His thinking had changed completely within twenty-four hours. 'I need to speak to the police,' he said mid-morning on Thursday. 'And I want a solicitor.'

The uniformed man sighed and nodded. How often had he heard those words from first-time offenders. They thought they were hard, that they wouldn't talk, but once they'd had a taste of prison life, and its food, it was a different story. And this wasn't even prison, only a remand centre. 'I'll see what I can do,' he said, well aware that the police believed Johnson might have information regarding a murder, might even have committed it himself.

It was two thirty in the afternoon when Ian arrived and was shown into the room where Luke was waiting. With him was a suited female with spiky, cropped blonde hair. 'I'm Angie Patterson,' she said, extending a hand.

'DCI Roper, Rickenham Green CID.' Ian shook the smooth ringless hand. 'I believe your client has something to say to us.'

She nodded and glanced at Luke who blinked nervously. 'Just tell Inspector Roper exactly what you told me, Luke,' she instructed.

Ian sat down wondering if he was about to hear some fabricated tale intended to get Luke out of trouble.

'That night, the night the lady at the restaurant was killed. I was there. We both were. On the Tuesday evening.'

At last. Thank you, God, Ian said silently. He decided to

let him tell it in his own way and not to interrupt with questions. It would all become clear in the end.

'We knew that the restaurant wasn't going to open until Saturday and that there was a private party on Friday because we'd seen the piece in the paper. Terry had been watching the place. He knew there was no one there at night, he also knew they'd had a large delivery of frozen food. You'd think it would all be fresh, somewhere like that,' he added unexpectedly. 'He said, because of its location, it would be a piece of cake to break in. I mean, no one expects a restaurant to be done, do they? And it wasn't as if there would've been any money as it wasn't even open yet so no one could have anticipated it.' He looked at Ian as if he was waiting for him to confirm Terry's logic.

Ian nodded. He had a name, or part of a name. Terry. And he had witnesses who had been at La Pêche on the relevant night. He prayed for a description or a car registration.

'We were behind a car, it turned in and parked in the car-park. A woman got out, it must have been her, the one who was killed, except we didn't know that then. We didn't know what to do. See, Terry thought we could get in round the back and that it would be better in daylight in case anyone saw the van. If they noticed they'd think it belonged to workmen doing some last-minute jobs.

'We stopped on the road and waited but she didn't come out. Anyway, a few minutes later another car pulled in and that's when we knew we had to forget it, at least for that night.'

'So you saw Julie Watson enter the premises. What time would this have been?'

'Like I said, it was still daylight. About half seven, something like that.'

'Right. And the second car arrived just afterwards. Did you see the driver?'

'Not really. It was a man, though.'

'Did you notice the make of car?'

'No. I've never owned one, I'm not into them. Terry might've done, though.'

'Does this Terry have a surname?'

'Noble. Terry Noble.' He had said it, there was no turning back now.

Frozen food. La Pêche was mainly a fish restaurant but there were other meals on the menu. Jim Hurst had told him that most of the fish and all of the vegetables would be fresh but it would not be economical to order meat daily because fewer people would choose it. The more exotic species of fish tended to be seasonal but could not be bought in small quantities. These, Ian surmised, were the ones Jim Hurst would have purchased frozen. 'Thank you. So you and Terry planned to break in and steal this delivery of frozen food. You were thwarted that night so instead of waiting until later or returning at another time, you went to the Poplars the following night. Why was that?'

Luke looked more uncomfortable than ever. It was one thing dropping Terry in it but Jo was another matter. 'Because we'd had some money on account and we'd promised the delivery by Wednesday night.'

'So you had a buyer in advance. Would you care to tell me who that was?' This was a different version of events from Johnson's initial one.

'Do I have to?'

Angie Patterson, who had remained silent, now advised her client. 'I think it's best if you do, Luke. Any help you can give the police is bound to go in your favour when it comes to sentencing.'

'Okay. His name's Jo Chan – well, that's what he calls himself. He owns the China Garden takeaway in Saxborough Road.'

Ian knew it. The few meals he had had from there were no better than average. 'Have you done this sort of thing before? Supplied him?'

'No. I swear to you, it's the first time I've ever done anything like this. I don't know why I agreed to it in the first place. I'd done my mum a bad turn and I wanted the money to repay her. Terry made it all sound so easy.'

'Do you know where we can find this Terry?'

'I don't know where he lives, I've only ever met him in the King's Head.'

'How did you get involved with him?'

'He was at the bar. He noticed that I rolled my own cigarettes and asked if I was interested in buying some cheap tobacco.'

'And, naturally, you said yes. And the source of the tobacco?' But Ian already knew the answer. It would be interesting to see what was stored above the Chinese take-away. And they would have to tread carefully, there must be no hint of racism here. Luke confirmed what he had guessed. Ian decided to send Eddie or Grant back to the King's Head. They were both already known to the land-lord, who had proved to be co-operative and who had said he didn't want trouble in his pub. He should, therefore, be only too pleased to have a local villain removed. And if Terry Noble drank there it was highly likely that he lived in the neighbourhood. Luke had not been much help as a witness to Julie Watson's murder but he might have pro-vided the answer to another problem on their books. They had known that illegal tobacco was coming into the area but so far had been unable to find either the source or the supplier. 'Thank you, Luke. I'm sure everything you've told me will be borne in mind when it comes to your future.' Ian stood. 'Nice to have met you, Miss Patterson.' She smiled but did not otherwise respond. Maybe he had offended her by not calling her Ms, an appellation Ian abhorred.

Back in the car he radioed the new information through to the station and requested that Eddie Roberts went immediately to the King's Head. Inspector Grant was with Cassandra Maguire's family, trying to build up a picture of her short life.

Driving back, he hoped that Terry Noble had been more observant than Luke, who had been a fool to have become involved with the man. But Luke was weak and easily manipulated. In all probability he had learned his lesson.

'Back again?' the landlord of the King's Head said when Eddie Roberts pushed open the door. Fortunately it was Thursday. The pub only opened all day from Thursdays to Sundays. At four in the afternoon there were several customers. One or two were in overalls and had probably knocked off for the day after an early start. In one corner sat an elderly couple studying a crossword.

'A pint, if I recall right?'

'No thanks. I wouldn't mind a coffee, though.' There was a machine on the counter behind the bar that produced espresso and cappuccino. Eddie thought it a bit sophisticated for the area.

'Ordinary filter or something else?'

'No. A large espresso, please.' Eddie slid one pound eighty on to the bar. 'What can you tell me about Terry Noble?'

'Not a lot. I know who he is but he's new around here. Been coming in for about four or five months, but not on a regular basis.' He paused. 'You were asking about Luke Johnson last time. I've seen them in conversation a couple of times. Perhaps I should've mentioned it. Not that I'd call them friends, really.

'Anyway, he lives in that block behind the pub. Don't know the number of the flat, but I overheard him say that his front window looks down on to the back of the pub. That's as much as I can tell you. I don't know what he does for a living, or if he's even got a job. Never been in at lunchtime, though, so he might be employed.'

'So you haven't heard any rumours about him?'

'Not a thing. And I'd tell you if I had.'

Eddie raised his cup again. 'Nice coffee.'

'We sell a lot of it during the morning sessions. Lunchtime business is good, me and the wife have been trying to build it up.' He indicated the menu chalked on a board on the wall. It looked appetizing. 'We get a lot of older people in for lunch, those who like to lock themselves in at night, and it keeps us ticking over nicely.'

'What does this Noble look like?'

'Medium height, dark hair cut very short and he wears glasses.'

'Thanks. I'm off. If Noble does come in there's no need to mention we were asking after him.'

'You can count on me.' The landlord put Eddie's cup and saucer in the washer and wiped the already spotless counter with a cloth.

Outside Eddie glanced at the sky and decided to make his call from the car. The drizzle had turned into steady rain and although it wasn't cold there was a noticeable drop in the temperature. There were many ways of discovering where someone lived but simply asking was one of the easiest. He requested back-up. Luke Johnson had proved no threat to anyone but Terry Noble was an unknown quantity.

At ten minutes to five Eddie and Alan Campbell stood outside the door of Noble's flat. It was on the top floor and would have a panoramic view of the desolation below it but also of the distant fields that spreading development had not yet reached. Eddie knocked loudly enough to be heard over a television if one had been playing. There was no response. 'We'll wait,' he said. 'If he's out at work he ought to be back soon.'

They went back down to the car by way of the stairs. Rain streamed down the windscreen partially obscuring their view but not to the extent that they wouldn't see a man walking towards the front entrance. The whole place looked even more dismal and depressing under the low grey sky.

'If he knows we arrested Luke he might not come back,' Alan pointed out. 'How long shall we wait?'

'A bit longer yet.' Eddie didn't think Noble would know. There had not been time for it to have been reported in the paper and he was certain Mrs Johnson would not have gone around telling people. The word would be out in time, of course, but for the moment Noble should be none the wiser.

One or two people came and went but no one fitting the brief description the landlord had given. They were about to give up when Alan said, 'Is that him?'

'It could be.' Hurrying towards the entrance, a folded newspaper held over his head, was a dark-haired man wearing glasses. They got out of the car and followed him. 'Mr Noble?' Eddie said.

The man turned. His glasses were speckled with moisture. He took them off and stared myopically at his interceptors. 'Yes?'

'We're police officers.' Noble's face fell. He looked even more sick when he learned that he was under arrest but allowed himself to be handcuffed to Alan and led to the car without a fuss.

'Has he been booked in?' Ian asked when they had returned.

'Yes.'

'Then let's ask our Mr Noble some questions.'

An hour and a half later they had obtained a confession from Noble concerning his part in the aborted break-in at La Pêche and the successful one at the Poplars. They also had the make of the car seen pulling into the restaurant car-park, but no number, and a vague description of the man driving it.

Noble was duly charged and another case was almost concluded. As Ian pulled on his raincoat ready to go home he felt satisfied that something had been achieved that day. At that moment Greg Grant and Scruffy Short were on their way to the China Garden to bring in Jo Chan, if, as Luke Johnson had suggested, that was his name. With them were two uniformed officers armed with a search warrant.

Just in time he realized he had not warned Moira that he would be late. Not that late, it was only six thirty. He picked up the phone and spoke to her. 'I'll be about another hour,' he said. 'I'm buying a drink by way of celebration.'

'You've got him?'

'No. Not yet. I'll tell you about it later.'

Alan Campbell, Brenda Gibbons and Ian hurried through the rain to the Feathers. They would all be late home but it was traditional to share a drink and discuss the case when progress had been made. It was a time for unwinding before going home to a different world where no one could be expected to understand their work or the comradeship which came with it.

By the time Ian was ready for bed he was aware that there had been no more telephone calls and no attempt had been made to enter the homes of either Pamela Richards or Janice King. Janice had been out, briefly, to shop and to buy a newspaper. According to the man tailing her she had shown no obvious signs that she knew she was being followed closely. All was quiet. All except for the fact that Matthew Watson owned a car the same make and colour as the one described by Terry Noble which had pulled into the car-park behind Julie Watson's. And who else would she willingly let in if not her ex-husband?

By now Watson would be seated in one of the interview rooms with a lot of explaining to do. And that, Ian concluded as he pulled the duvet up around his ears, is precisely why all is quiet.

Chapter Fifteen

PC Anna Stevenson watched as Maggie Telford packed an overnight bag, wishing she owned such an extensive wardrobe as that of her charge.

'I can't wait to get away,' Maggie said as she folded a rose pink dress and packed it carefully. On top of that she placed underwear and a satin and lace nightdress in apple green and cream.

'I can see that.' Anna smiled. Maggie's excitement was obvious.

'It feels as though I've been cooped up for ever.'

Anna was aware of the connection between Luke Johnson and Terry Noble and La Pêche. She also knew that Jo Chan had now been charged on two counts. He sold the stolen food over the counter of his takeaway and the tobacco under it. Several of his relatives had been charged with smuggling the tobacco in. Matthew Watson had also been picked up the previous night but she did not know the outcome of that interview. She had simply been told to carry on as instructed, which is exactly what she was doing. She would drive Maggie to the Grand in Saxborough, ensure both she and Brian Schofield were in the car and safely on their way then return to her normal duties until it was time to collect Maggie on Monday morning. It was only ten o'clock, there was an hour and a half before they needed to set off.

By now Anna had learned a lot of Maggie's history: her career, her unsuccessful marriage followed by the divorce, the occasional men along the way and now Brian. 'Do you love him?' Anna had asked, wondering if she ought to have been so personal.

'Yes, I think I do. I can't explain it, he just makes me feel good.'

'Would you ever get married again?'

Maggie had laughed and shook her head. 'I don't know. Once bitten, as they say. Besides, I'm used to living alone, I'd find it very hard to share the house with someone again. Oh, I didn't mean to be rude. Having you here is different and it's only temporary. No, I've come to enjoy my freedom too much for that.' She paused. 'I think,' she added with a smile.

The subject had been dropped. Maggie had not asked Anna to volunteer any personal details in return and Anna had appreciated her tact.

They drank coffee and waited for the time to pass. At eleven thirty-five Anna opened the door, peered into the rain and declared it was safe to leave.

'Not much of a start to the summer,' Maggie commented as she fastened her seat belt. 'I hope it's better than this where we're going.'

Anna drove in silence. The traffic was heavy and water ran down the windscreen in sheets. Total concentration was required. When she pulled up outside the Grand Hotel they saw Brian standing beneath its portals waiting for them. On the drive in front stood a car. He pointed to it and came down the steps to meet them. Maggie got out of the unmarked police car and walked towards Brian's, an umbrella over her head.

'At last,' he said as he opened the passenger door for her. 'You've had an awful time. I'll try and make it up to you.' He went round to the other side, got in and started the engine, waved to Anna, then pulled away.

They stopped once for petrol and a second time for tea and scones which they ate by a log fire in a tiny tea-room. It was no longer raining when they left. Water still dripped from the trees but overhead the sky was blue.

Once they'd booked into the hotel they went upstairs to

change for dinner. 'It's wonderful here,' Maggie said as they sipped a pre-dinner drink.

'I know. If the weather's like this in the morning, we'll go for a long walk and find a pub to have lunch. I just want you to relax, to forget everything for a day or so.'

'You, too,' Maggie said, realizing the strain Brian had also been under, worrying about her and work and then the long drive. It was no wonder he was unable to make love to her but fell asleep almost immediately they were in bed.

'Oh, no,' Ian said. He and Moira were shopping for a present for Moira's mother's birthday. Ian normally avoided shops but he was extremely fond of Philippa who was an older version of his wife and long widowed. They had spent Saturday morning at home then had a drink in the Crown before venturing out once the rain had stopped.

'It's all right,' Moira said, understanding his frustration at having to answer his mobile phone in the middle of a department store.

He went to the stairwell and took the call there. When he returned to where Moira was waiting his face was grim. 'We made a mistake,' he said. 'We should never have let Maggie Telford out of our sight.'

'Oh, Ian, what's happened?' Moira ran a hand through her fair hair, fearing the worst.

'She's disappeared.'

Disappeared, not dead. 'Do you have to go in?'

'No, they're dealing with it up there. They've got all the details.'

'Look, I can get something for Mum during my lunch hour on Monday. Shall we go and have some coffee?'

Ian nodded and followed her towards the staircase which led up to the coffee shop. Once there they queued at the counter then Ian carried their tray to a vacant table which overlooked the busy street below. Moira knew he wanted to talk about it, to relieve himself of some of the guilt he must be feeling.

'She went away with Schofield. He'd been cleared for the two nights of the murders. Anyway, the hotel in Cumbria have confirmed they checked in, ate dinner and came down again for breakfast. The waitress who served them said they were smiling and holding hands over the table. They went out about ten, but no one knows where, only that they were expected back for dinner. Schofield reserved a table for eight o'clock before they left.

'He rang us from a village. He said they'd been walking and decided to drive somewhere for lunch. He parked in the car-park but when he returned to the car with the pay-and-display ticket she'd disappeared. He waited, assuming she'd gone to use the Ladies opposite or had wandered off to look in shop windows, but when she didn't come back he called us.'

'Not the local police?'

'No. I suppose he thought we'd take more notice as they didn't know the circumstances. We've been in touch with them now and they've instigated a full-scale search.'

'They must have been followed.'

'No. I don't think so. He would have had to be on their tails since Maggie left her house and you can't just snatch someone in the little time it takes to buy a parking ticket. Besides, she'd have screamed or attracted attention to herself in some way if that was the case.'

'So what do you think happened?'

'She might be on her way back, they might have had a row.'

'But she'd wait until they returned to the hotel so she could arrange transport if he refused to drive her back.'

Ian sighed. 'Yes. I know that really. Maybe the killer did get wind of where she was, perhaps she saw him, realized who it was and took off. No. That doesn't ring true either.'

'Then what?'

'I don't know.' Ian sipped his coffee, Moira made no

196

comment when he added sugar instead of the sweeteners she offered him.

'Do you think he killed her?'

'If he did he's very cool. He'd be the obvious suspect. And he rang us almost at once.' Unless he killed her before he reached the village, unless he'd already disposed of the body earlier, Ian couldn't bear to think of it.

Moira looked around. The coffee shop was busy with mid-afternoon tea and coffee drinkers. The groups and couples mainly consisted of women but there were a few men around. And a screaming child, she noticed. 'What happened with Julie Watson's ex-husband?'

'He was questioned again but he refuses to budge. He swears he knows nothing about her murder and was nowhere near La Pêche on the night in question. His girlfriend alibis him, but, as they say, she would, wouldn't she? Forensics have got his car. If he was there they should be able to match the grit from the car-park or find something to incriminate him. We're still holding him, but it can't be for much longer unless we charge him.'

He looked pale and worried and Moira knew he held himself responsible for both Cassandra Maguire's death and Maggie's disappearance. But surely Superintendent Thorne must have given permission for Maggie's weekend away? 'Look, why don't we have a night out?' she suggested. If they stayed in he would be hovering by the telephone, brooding. 'Why don't I book us a table at the Duke of Clarence? It's ages since we've been there.'

'Yes. Let's.'

'Give me your phone and I'll do it now. I know the number.' Ian handed it over. Moira made the arrangements and handed it back.

'What is it?' His wife was frowning.

'I'm not sure. Well, you heard what I said, didn't you?'

'Not really.'

'Well, I asked for a table for two for eight thirty and gave our name. They can fit us in, by the way. But, Ian, they asked for our telephone number.'

'Yes, that's normal practice with restaurants. Jesus, Moira, I see what you mean.'

'Is it possible? I mean, we go to the Duke of Clarence on special occasions or when we feel like treating ourselves. The Grand in Saxborough's that sort of place, too, isn't it? Somewhere you go for a treat, not somewhere where most people could afford to go regularly, so those women would hardly have been likely to include it in their lists if they'd only been there once.'

But Ian wasn't listening, he was already dialling a number. 'Get on to Janice King, Pamela Richards and Helen Potter immediately,' he said to Scruffy Short who answered the phone in the general office. 'Find out if they've ever eaten or stayed at the Grand in Saxborough. If so, get on to Cumbria and tell them to arrest Brian Schofield.' He ended the call and looked at Moira, shaking his head. 'I can't believe you sometimes. One of us should have thought of that. If it is the case, of course. Do me a favour, go and get us another coffee. I'll sit here and wait for Short to ring back.'

Moira wondered what the other customers would think of her husband's antisocial behaviour until she realized she had also made a call on the mobile.

It was fifteen minutes before Short rang back. Moira only heard Ian's few gruff words. 'Yes,' he said. 'Yes. Okay. Thanks.' With a sigh of satisfaction he switched the phone off and put it in his pocket.

'Well?'

'Pamela Richards has eaten there on two occasions. Once with her parents when they came to stay, once with the manager of one of the Saxborough stores for whom she had worked. On the first occasion she booked the table herself. Helen Potter took her boyfriend there for a farewell dinner before he went off to Africa, it was one of the rare times he allowed her to pay, and Janice King ate there

198

on a friend's birthday, again the table was booked in her name.' Ian shook his head in disbelief.

'God, it's so obvious now. He saw them, probably even spoke to them. In an establishment like that they make a point of knowing who the host or hostess is. In fact the women probably said something along the lines of "I've booked a table in the name of," whatever, when they arrived. All Schofield had to do was to look at the reservations book and make a note of their number. And then he could check their addresses in the phone book.'

'But one of them was ex-directory.'

'Yes. Maggie Telford. But she gave him her number herself, just as she did with Smithson.'

'I still don't see why he should risk harming Maggie when it would be so obvious. Besides, you said he had an alibi for both killings.'

'Alibis we'll need to look into more carefully now. Come on, let's go. There's nothing I can do until the Cumbrian police have done their bit.'

They were getting ready to go out that evening when the telephone rang. Ian almost knocked Moira over as he rushed across the bedroom to answer the extension on his side of the bed. Maggie Telford was alive and well. She had, indeed, got out of the car whilst Brian's back was turned. She had run to the small taxi rank across the street and asked to be driven to the nearest police station. It had taken her some time to convince them that all she was saying was true and that she was not suffering from paranoid delusions. The officers at the small station where she had sat answering questions were not then aware that Rickenham Green had been on to their regional headquarters.

'It'll wait until the morning. Someone else can deal with things tonight,' Ian said, catching sight of the glum expression on Moira's face. 'Come on, let's go and have ourselves a lovely meal.'

Ian knew nothing more than the few details he had learned over the telephone, which, in themselves, didn't add up to much. But tomorrow both Maggie Telford and Brian Schofield would be back in Rickenham Green and maybe then they could start fitting in the missing pieces.

It was Maggie they spoke to first. Ian and Brenda listened to what she had to say.

'We were out walking. It'd been a lovely weekend up until then. Brian started telling me a bit about his childhood, how he'd never known his father and that his mother had neglected him, how much he'd loved her even so. He said she was beautiful with long, dark hair like mine and that I reminded him of her. He caught hold of my hair and wound it around his wrist. He didn't hurt me or anything but it was then I began to feel a bit scared and a bit angry as well. I thought we had a relationship, I didn't want to be some mother substitute.'

Brenda said nothing. She could understand the man's feelings. Her own childhood had many similarities to his.

'We were in the middle of nowhere so I tried not to let him see I was disturbed. He said, "You'd never laugh at me like she did, would you, Maggie?" The last thing I felt like doing was laughing. "No matter what I did for her she ignored me. Then there was Lizzie. That woman broke my heart, too." He stopped talking then but there was a weird look on his face. "Just please don't ever laugh at me," he said again.

'From what he'd said I got the impression that his mother may have been a prostitute. Anyway I suddenly wondered about him, about his wife, and if, despite what he told me, he actually hated his mother.' She paused. 'Now I'm back here this is probably going to sound fanciful, but it crossed my mind that he might have hated anyone who resembled her. You told me all the women receiving those telephone calls were dark.' She paused, aware of what she had said.

'Oh, God, poor Brian. What have I done to him? I'm

sorry, I panicked, I really began to believe he might have killed those women.'

Neither Brenda nor Ian interrupted her. They both knew that Brian Schofield had been married. 'Excuse me a minute,' Ian said. There was something more to be looked into. The disappearance of Schofield's wife five years ago. They had previously checked this out and his neighbours and family and Lizzie's friends had confirmed his story. There had been a stream of other men and she had finally run off with one of them. So they said. But now there was another possibility. And it fitted the pattern of a serial killer. One murder, just the one, and then the acceleration of killings. Brian Schofield's heart may have been broken but Maggie Telford's was about to be.

'You can go home,' Ian told her when he returned. 'You'll be safe now but would you like Anna Stevenson to go with you?'

'No. I'll be fine. I think I'd like to spend some time on my own now.'

'We'll arrange a lift.'

Maggie smiled wanly. 'Thank you.'

With the investigation of Lizzie Schofield's disappearance under way Ian went to report to Superintendent Thorne. He didn't want to speak to Schofield but he wasn't sure why, maybe it was because of his own guilt because he had not looked at the case logically, maybe it was because he was sure he knew what the outcome of that interview would do to Maggie. Short and Brenda would be with him now.

'I really don't understand what all this is about,' Schofield said. 'I mean, one minute we were having a great time then suddenly she runs away from me. I really don't know what I did to upset her or even why I'm here.'

They questioned him for hours, taking it in turns, each knowing exactly when to take over. Brian Schofield's story never altered; he knew nothing about the telephone calls, apart from what Maggie had told him and the one she had received in his presence, and he certainly hadn't killed anyone.

'Your wife. Lizzie. She disappeared five years ago and has never been heard of again. Can you explain that?' Brenda asked him.

Schofield ran a hand through his soft, fair hair and sighed. 'I don't know where you got that idea. She didn't disappear, she went off with someone else. And she did come back, just the once. She said she wanted a reconciliation but by then I realized she was never going to change. She'd been dumped that time, it was money she wanted, not me. That was one of the reasons I moved out of the area once I'd got over her. Our marriage was over. I didn't want her to find me again.' He laughed. It was a bitter sound. 'So you see, I'm still married. When I met Maggie I knew I'd have to try to trace her so I could get a divorce but I suppose I've blown it now.'

'He's a bloody good actor, I'll say that for him,' Short commented when Schofield had been returned to his holding cell.

'I don't know . . .'

'What don't you know, my lovely?'

'It just doesn't feel right.'

And within an hour she was proved right.

Maggie felt awful. She had acted like an hysterical fool. It was good to be home but she didn't believe the Chief Inspector, she didn't feel safe. The doors and windows were locked as she sat staring out into the quiet street. The sun was shining and a bee banged stupidly against the window pane. When the doorbell rang she jumped. Assuming the police had decided she did need protection after all, she went to open the door. Her smile faded immediately.

'May I come in?'

'No.' She shoved the door closed but he was too strong

for her. Her heart thumped and her legs felt weak. She couldn't even scream.

With her life at stake and nothing to lose, she reached for the bronze nude which stood on the hall table beside a vase of flowers.

As he reached for her Maggie tightened her grip on the statue.

'Well,' she said with a smile which took him so much by surprise that he stopped moving. In those few seconds Maggie drew back her arm and slammed the nude into the side of his head. Blood spurted as she ran for the phone. Choking on tears and terror she dialled 999.

'You look absolutely exhausted,' Moira told Ian when he pushed open the kitchen door on Sunday evening and leaned against the jamb.

'I am.' He summoned up a smile. 'And thirsty and hungry.'

Moira had long given up preparing a traditional Sunday lunchtime roast and they preferred to eat in the evening anyway. 'Beer?'

He nodded and sat down. He was half-way down the glass before he spoke again. 'We were right from the start. We had him and we let him go. A life could've been saved, maybe even two.'

'It wasn't Schofield?'

'No. True, his wife did disappear but it was as everyone said at the time. There were other men. She took off with one of them but it didn't work out. She's been traced. She's living with someone else now and working as a supermarket cashier.

'You had the right idea, Moira, about how someone could get their telephone numbers and addresses but we overlooked one very important aspect. Smithson works in insurance. We knew that, of course, but we also knew none of the women was insured with his company. What we didn't check was whether they had been with the previous

203

outfit he worked for.' Another oversight. How many mistakes had they made?

'So it was Smithson.'

'Yes. Until a year or so ago he was a partner in a small broker's outfit selling car and house insurance. Because of the introduction of direct selling there were financial problems so Smithson decided to get out. Meanwhile his relationship with Isobel Evans, as she was then, had gone wrong. Again, we should've seen it. There hasn't been anyone else since. She'd married and moved away and no one would tell him where, he couldn't get to her but there were other women like her, women on his books who looked like her. He was obsessed with her and, in his eyes, she'd made a fool of him.

'Of the six women Maggie Telford was the exception. She actually went out with Smithson. He had never sold her a policy, nor had she been to his old office. She came across him at a charity bash. We now know that Cassandra Maguire once made the mistake of laughing when he suggested she might like to have a drink with him. Back then she had changed her car to a newer more upmarket model and needed to make adjustments to her policy. All six women had dealings of some sort with him at his previous job.'

'But none of them mentioned this?'

'No. Why should they have done? The firm went bust, by which time Smithson had moved on anyway and they had made other insurance arrangements. They had no way of knowing that Smithson had taken with him the names, numbers and addresses of the clients who reminded him of Isobel.

'After Maggie dropped him he pestered her, but she knew who was calling. She might've been safe if she'd continued seeing him. The shrink believes he transferred his obsession to Maggie. He's sick, of course, but what started as a game, a way of frightening those who'd rejected him, wasn't enough. He had lost Isobel, then Maggie, and was convinced they were all laughing at him. Maggie had also left him for another man, just as he believed Isobel had done.'

'And it would have been easy for him, in that line of work, to acquire details of their personal circumstances,' Moira added.

'Exactly. For contents to be insured certain security measures are required. A simple question like "Do you live alone? If so I suggest you get a burglar alarm, a chain on the door," that sort of thing. Their replies would tell him all he needed to know.

'He thought he was clever. He rang Pam Richards with a warning. We outguessed him, we knew it would be one of the others but we thought it would be Janice King. And then this thing with Schofield threw us completely off the track.'

'No wonder. But I can understand Maggie Telford's point of view. She must've been terrified when Schofield starting talking the way he did.' Moira got up and refilled Ian's glass, realizing she hadn't got a drink herself. There was no point in starting the meal, Ian wouldn't be ready to eat until he had talked this through. 'Why did Julie Watson let him into the restaurant?'

'He'd checked that the women were still at the addresses he'd got and followed them, watching and waiting for the opportunity when he could catch them alone. Julie was the first. He remembered her as quiet and couldn't be sure she'd let him in so he followed her to La Pêche, knocked on the window and told her he represented the company insuring the restaurant. He produced a genuine card from his present firm and said he had arranged to meet the owner there that night. If Julie remembered him she'd also remember he worked in insurance. She did remember him and that's why she let him in.

'We don't know if he went there with the intention of killing her, he hadn't taken a weapon with him but he would have known there would be kitchen knives. Perhaps he simply hoped to persuade her to go out with him. But he did kill her, and by now he'd got the taste for it.'

Ian then explained how he had tricked Cassandra Maguire, how he had claimed to work in market research and got her to meet him in the pub.

Ian sipped his beer and wiped his mouth with the back of his hand. 'He worked on the basis that now they had met she was more likely to let him in. Maggie was his next target although he had no idea the women were by then under police protection. He rang her several times over the weekend but realized she must've gone away and that she would probably return on Sunday, which she did, albeit a day earlier than she had intended. That's when he made his move.'

Moira took a sip of wine. 'And he would also have assumed that Maggie had no idea that there was any connection between her and the murdered women because she had actually been out with him and knew it was him who had been telephoning her.'

'Quite. He'd been expecting a cool reception but not the one he got. She gave him quite a whack and a dose of concussion.'

'What about the car? You thought it was Julie's husband's?'

'Smithson's was in for servicing. He had one of those agreements whereby the garage lend you one until the work's done. It was pure coincidence it was the same make as Watson's. And Smithson was clever, he touched nothing. He admitted that when he grabbed the knife from the rack to kill Julie he had his handkerchief wrapped around his hand. With Cass he kept his hands in his pockets until the moment he strangled her. He picked up a set of keys, locked the door and drove her car away. He wasn't too worried about forensic evidence. It rained again on Saturday night, he wore a cap.'

'I don't understand.'

'That lessened the chances of stray hairs. Anyway, he dumped the car, made his way home and got rid of every article of clothing he was wearing.

'Well, that's quite enough of that. Is there any food,

woman, or does a man have to starve in his own house?'

'A little more respect, if you don't mind, or you will starve.'

Ian smiled but it would be a long time before he would be able to forgive himself. It was doubtful they could have done anything to prevent Julie Watson's death but a second life had been lost needlessly through a lack of logical thought processes. And, Ian realized, in a way Smithson had had his own sort of logic. It must never happen again.

Brenda Gibbons was furious with herself and nothing Andrew said could make her feel any better. 'You're a team,' he told her, 'the responsibility wasn't yours alone. Come on, let's go for a walk before you explode.'

She apologized. Pulling on a jacket she followed him out of the door and stomped the first few hundred yards through the marram grass until the sound of the sea, ebbing and flowing, soothed her.

'We got the bastard,' Scruffy Short said as he disentangled himself from Nancy's warm, damp limbs. He had telephoned to see if she was free, driven over, rung her bell and led her straight to the bedroom by way of celebration. There was no remorse, no recriminations on his part. Mistakes had been made but the job was done.

Nancy flung back her hennaed hair and laughed. 'If this is what it does to you, I hope all your cases are equally successful. I think you can buy me dinner now.'

If he wanted a repeat performance later, Short knew he had no option but to agree. He stepped into the clothes that had lain on the floor in a heap, flipped his hair over the bald spot, slapped Nancy on her behind and grinned lasciviously as the bare dimpled flesh wobbled.

*   *   *

Maggie Telford was still shaken but at least it really was over now.

What worried her most was not the injuries she had inflicted upon Smithson but what she had done to Brian. If the situation was in reverse she doubted she would be able to forgive him his doubts and fears. Brenda Gibbons had rung to say that he had been released and had gone back to the Grand. All charges had been dropped.

She stood in the lounge in the dark. So Brian was back at the hotel. He was not on duty but he hadn't tried to contact her. She was near to tears, they should still have been together in the Lake District. Perhaps he had gone somewhere for the night. But he might be in his suite. With a trembling hand she picked up the receiver and rang the number now so familiar to her. 'May I speak to Brian Schofield?' she asked in a voice she barely recognized as her own. Did any of the blame lie with her? she wondered. Had she not lied to the police would things have been different? No, she had tried to point the finger at Smithson all along. Yes, but without involving herself. Selfish bitch, she thought as she was connected to Brian's suite. 'Hello, it's me. Maggie. Can we talk? Can you forgive me?'

There was a long silence. 'I've had plenty of time to think about it. Being charged with murder is not my idea of fun but I can understand how you must've felt. That thing with Smithson, I didn't take it seriously enough, nor did I realize how frightened you were and that you were bound to view everyone with suspicion, even me.'

'Oh, Brian.' She was crying with relief. Hot tears ran down her face. He understood, he was prepared to talk, she was in with a chance. For now that was enough.

And in the morning she would return to work and life would continue as normal. No, it could never be that again, but she would appreciate what she had. And she would always remember that there were two other women who no longer had the chance to do that.